Halcyon:
Faith

Episode I

of

The Halcyon's
Wake Chronicles

By Arbra Dale Triplett

Copyright © 2013, 2016 Arbra Creative Solutions

Phoenix, Arizona

Third Edition

ISBN-10:
0-692-70079-X
ISBN-13:
978-0-692-70079-2

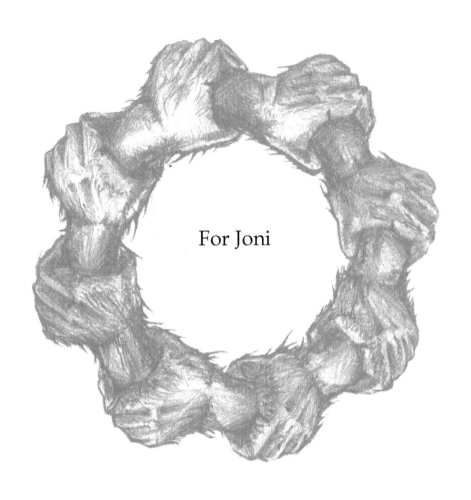

For Joni

Cover Illustrations: Sandra Johnson
Cover Design: SMAK Graphics

Table of Contents

Prologue

In four days, Halcyon would rise to the naked eye. Four days after that, the earth would be a greasy spot spread along the side of the galactic highway.

The quibbling over Halcyon's designation at the national observatory seemed trite. Who really cared if it couldn't truly be classified as a comet? A wavering ion tail, methodical movements dictated by unseen forces, a precise dust tail littering its break-neck cosmic path with glittering, amorphous crystals - bus-sized bread crumbs strewn across the vast panoply. Bigger than our friggin' moon and making a bee-line to earth at a pace the astronomical gurus couldn't even begin to compute. "Ludicrous speed," quipped a grad student, his *Space Balls* quote lost on the stoic faces surrounding him.

The greatest minds on the planet gazed slack-jawed at the approaching entity -deemed *Halcyon* by some sensationalizing, opportunistic White House journalist; quoting out of context our poetic President's heartfelt plea as he learned the perilous truth. *Dear God, please bring us once more upon halcyon days' doorstep.*

All NASA's scientists said with tremulous certainty was, "It appears to have originated in NGC-4565," followed by confident assertions of what they *did* know. "NGC-4565 is not unknown to us, a galaxy beyond our own, lying at a distance, in miles, of 117 followed by 18 zeros. Basically... one million years travel at the speed of light." To further placate the laymen, he added, "If we sent a message to the edge of NGC-4565, we'd be on hold for two million years waiting for a response."

"Then why didn't we see it coming sooner," shouted a reporter over the murmuring hubbub. The NASA spokesperson, a veteran of scrutiny stemming from various failures over decades as America clambered for the skies, visibly paled and reached for the podium to steady himself.

"We don't know," he said. "It's as if Halcyon... (he'd already given up fighting the name given by the press.)... logic and science tell us that Galileo, Newton and even Copernicus *should* have seen its approach, but its velocity alone defies our comprehension."

An older astronomer from the University of Wyoming, Professor Randall Vandenberg, the first to observe Halcyon, leaned forward to the microphone in front of him, his copious, wiry, salt-and-pepper beard bouncing slightly as he spoke. "A calm pond will remain calm until someone tosses in a rock. From that point of impact we can see the ripples spread across the surface. The ripples we measure across this galactic pond are measured by their luminescence, and Halcyon basically just splashed into our galaxy without giving us the simple courtesy of an advanced ripple."

Within twenty minutes of the globally televised conference, a ripple that *was* evident began, this one through the people of Earth. Global disbelief hung in a pregnant pause, followed by a thinly veiled panic. Fear fueled futile and hasty preparations, desperate efforts at defiance, a field mouse flipping off the descending falcon.

A few radical religious groups committed the token mass suicide; others rejoiced that salvation was near at hand, depending on what flavor of faith you ascribed to. Aboriginal tribes in Australia's Northern Territory converged on Mount Uluru (Ayers Rock to English speakers) supposedly to "greet the coming visitors." A crazed and sleep-deprived Zambian student from Lusaka earned his fifteen minutes of fame claiming Halcyon was merely an envoy from afar, that he had been conversing with the galactic travelers via his home-made radio telescope. Others simply partied like it was 1999.

With calmness the bespectacled Professor Vandenberg said, "Four days until Halcyon is visible to the naked eye -even in daylight. Four days after that, she'll roll right through us like a hot knife through butter. It's been fun, people... Peace." He'd flashed a hippie smile, a well-intentioned peace sign, then rose from the table and unhurriedly left the room, ignoring the reporter's pleas.

"Where are you going, Doctor?" asked one of his grad students hovering near the exit.

"To get very drunk, Thomas," came the chuckled reply. "Very

drunk indeed."

It was during his quest for alcoholic stupefaction that I met the esteemed Doctor. Five days had passed since the press conference. Five days and a lot of Scotch, from the looks of the disheveled professor. He was cozily embracing the bar of the Shangri-La hotel in Cocoa Beach, Florida. Drunkenness slightly glazed his intelligent eyes, a lucid gleam tinted with the redness of excess. "Comfortably numb," he assured me, offering up an unlit Cuban cigar from several boxes arrayed before him.

I hesitated briefly then took the proffered stogie.

"Hello, old friend," I muttered, spitting the butt end across the bar, "Guess the embargo doesn't mean a heck of a lot anymore, does it, Doc,"

"To all the vices, Skipper" he shouted, filling a tumbler of Scotch, splashing a few ice cubes into the mix and sliding it in front of me with a grand and practiced flourish. *Quite the accomplishment for a man confined to a restrictive pressure suit, this guy should have been a pilot.*

"Here's to swimmin' with bow-legged women, Doc," I toasted, sipping on the fiery, smooth, single malt. "But I ain't the Skipper, I sit in the right seat." The liquor warmed soothingly and I took a long draw on the smooth tobacco, "I hope to God we've got a tobacco farmer in this ragtag group."

The professor laughed his approval, refilling his own tumbler.

"I suppose that makes you the luckiest co-pilot on the planet," he said.

"I'll withhold judgment on that until we're well into orbit, Doc," I replied.

A young scientist and his wife sat at the end of the bar, quiet and serene over a bottle of wine. I remembered meeting both of them at the Christmas party last year.
Her face was the epitome of tranquility, and I thought how she reflected so much of how the general populous had faced the planet's demise. Sure, people went a little crazy. Who could honestly blame them?

Money meant nothing anymore. *Nothing* really mattered anymore. Enterprise and industry stopped in a flash. The maddened frenzy of anarchy didn't reach the fevered pitch most anticipated, though. The people might have sown a few well-deserved wild oats. It was the supposed leaders of the world that went postal on a global scale.

Israel snapped first. Their nukes turned Lebanon and most of Syria into a parking lot. Before news stopped coming from the barren region, headlines screamed of how the Israelis would face extinction "knowing their enemies were first vanquished." India and Pakistan followed suit, choosing to go out fighting -at least amongst themselves. The latest satellite images showed the first explosive plumes dotting the Korean peninsula, and America waited with fierce temerity, itchy fingers poised over active switches.

But China balked. And so did Russia. A tension lingered that could snap at the faintest fart on the breeze, and Halcyon still careened earthward. The professor puffed thoughtfully on his contraband stogie, motioning stiffly towards the heavens with an arm constrained by the rigid, bright-orange suit. The surreal nature of this bizarre scene could've been a broadway play titled "People Drinking in Space Suits."

"I'd watched the skies with interest initially like everyone," the professor said, glancing to the gathered fortunate few scattered throughout the bar. I glimpsed one couple getting naked in a darkened corner booth. *Why not*, I mused, sipping the Scotch.

"Hell, I found the blasted thing after all," the professor continued. It was becoming obvious the restraint he'd been holding onto was teetering atop a fine edge, the alcohol slowly winning over resolve. The wooziness would hit me, too, if I didn't slow the pace a bit.

"That why they gave you a seat?" I asked, not unkindly.

"I guess so," he wheezed, "that and my delicate delivery of doomsday to the world!" He laughed drunkenly, raising his glass and I clinked my tumbler dutifully against his.

"Heck of a finder's fee, Doc," I said soberly, then casually motioned towards the piled Cubans. "Better enjoy those while you can, sir."

A steady beep began to thrum at random locations throughout the bar, red LED lights on twenty different pagers going off, mine included. I looked at the display flashing "911" and I knew I'd consumed my last adult beverage on planet Earth.

China must have spread its cheeks wide and let that malodorous waft hit the breeze. It was time to get the hell out of Dodge. Our shuttle launch scheduled for tomorrow was leaving slightly ahead of schedule, it seemed. *Time to fish or cut bait.*

"You ready, Doc?" I asked, belting the last of the Scotch and rising from the bar.

"Let's do it," he replied, swaying slightly to his feet, reaching for his bottle of booze and snuffing out his stogie. When I knew he could walk under his own determined power, I headed toward the lobby with the rest of the revelers. The amorous couple in the corner booth remained entangled, obviously opting to face the music together naked. *Worse ways to go...*

The mission commander stood in the lobby, shooting me an appraising glance which I dismissed with a wave. The "eight hours from bottle to throttle" rule went out the window when that big chunk of the unknown from space arrived, although I knew this was one flight I didn't want to be grounded from.

"Don't worry, Commander," I said as we went through the lobby doors to the waiting helicopters. "I flew for Northwest, remember? We always fly better with a couple cocktails."

He shook his head and clapped me on the back, then looked all business, "The missiles are flying," he said, "China changed its mind. I guess if you spent all that money on fireworks, you'd want to shoot them off, too. We go the moment everyone gets tied down."

"Jesus," I whispered, briefly regretting the Scotch. *At least if I screw this one up, there won't be anyone around to gripe about it.*

I climbed aboard the first Huey with the Commander, the drunken astronomer clambering in with a gentle shove from the astrophysicist-turned-instant-crew-chief, desperately clutching his pilfered bottle of Scotch close to his chest. *Billions on the planet and we're saving Otis the drunk.* The helo lifted with a nod from the Commander; three more NASA choppers taking off in succession behind us.

The hotel that had hosted every generation of astronaut since Gemini faded quickly away, smoldering remains of the interstate carpet bombed yesterday to ward off the masses pointing a charred and rubble strewn finger towards the cape. There was only one way off this rock and everyone knew it. The threat of global extinction pretty much redefined the food chain, giving a whole new meaning to 'class distinction'.

As we increased altitude and sped for the cape, I tapped the Commander's shoulder and pointed to the eastern horizon. Twelve plumes of steam and smoke streaked across the sky heading south and east. He leaned over and yelled loudly over the

Huey's pulsating thrum, "They're from the *Dallas*. She's been sitting right off the coast. We've got zero time to light this candle, Amigo." The *Dallas* was a Los Angeles class submarine, obviously playing its role in the mutually assured destruction scenario, launching its devastating payload to global targets of opportunity. *Check, please; I've got a thing...*

Beyond the streaming missiles, the growing visage of Halcyon loomed menacingly, its swirling surface clearly visible through the amber twilight. *Talk about being between a rock and a hard place.*

The helicopters approached the shuttle *Discovery*, hauled out of moth-balls a week ago and primed for launch since early yesterday, awaiting some of the more precious "cargo," namely the President and whatever cronies had cajoled one last chance at living, conning their way aboard the last train out of town. The lead chopper set down next to an armored hum-vee, unmanned but nevertheless lethal, no one would approach the shuttle without first tasting the lead from automated .50 cal machine guns and Mark-19 grenade launchers. *You definitely need a ticket to ride this baby.*

The chosen evacuees leapt from the helos, bending low beneath the dwindling rotor blast as the turbines wound down and moved towards the gantry that would transport them up to the shuttles crew door, then begin the long shuffle downward to the modified seating in the cargo bay.

Forty-seven souls, including the crew, made up the complement. Checklists normally adhered to with rigid discipline were hastily plowed through. If the shuttle had been equipped with a simple "go" button, I would have punched it once everyone was on board. *Stow your tray tables, ladies and germs; it's time to dance.*

A team of twelve engineers made up the contingent of launch control. *Brave men, one and all.* They knew all was lost and figured a lifetime wearing pocket protectors and thick-rimmed glasses would mean so much more in the grand scheme of things if only they could guarantee the last vestiges of humanity made it off the planet. Their only request had been to jot down their names as the saviors of the species. *No prob, if we get off of this soon-to-be-glowing rock.*

I finished up the hasty and highly modified checklist protocol with the shuttle Commander, Colonel Jim Garner, mentally praying Alan Shepard's infamous words over and over. *"Dear God, don't let me foul this up."* Although the esteemed naval man had used an expletive decidedly more severe, truer words were still never spoken.

The nerd saviors of mankind punched the correct buttons and *Discovery* thrummed to life, clambering upwards against gravity and slipping through the skies *truly* for the last time: million years of evolution fleeing a sinking ship.

The shuttle boosters fired, expended and slipped off into the atmosphere, no somber words of farewell from launch control, and nobody sitting in Houston to guide us once we reached orbit. Just eerie silence broken only by the Commander and I ticking off checklist items.

We hit the orbit that would put us in position to rendezvous with the International Space Station, rolled the shuttle on its back, the full measure of the devastation unfolding "above" us on the earth's surface as we sped rearward in excess of 17,000 mph.

President Bielski, his wife and the two young scientists from the bar were strapped in behind us on the flight deck, two more crew-members directly below us, all of us sealed separately from the shuttle's vast cargo bay. "My God," the President sighed, "What have we done?"

Europe rolled into view, at least what was visible through the maelstrom wreaking havoc on Earth's atmosphere. The perpetual *grayness* that swept over the continent in roiling clouds thankfully blanketed the devastation below, ashen blinders for the folly of man. Even if Halcyon managed to drift by mockingly, sparing earth, life wouldn't touch that bleak surface for a thousand years.

"Commander, I guess that now is as good a time as any," the President said solemnly. "May God forgive me."

The Commander let out an audible sigh over the intercom, an unwilling affirmation to a grim order. I eyed the Commander with keen puzzlement and watched in horror as he began the sequence to open the cargo bay doors. Normally one of the first things accomplished once we hit orbit to charge shuttle systems with solar energy - but not with a cargo of VIP's stacked like cordwood in the back.

"I told them I'd get them to space," the President said, "beyond that... no assurances."

The rapid decompression echoed through the hatch separating the flight deck from the cargo space, and the

Commander released the clamps holding the passenger seating to the shuttles deck. The platform slowly rose into the cold reaches of space, a hearse with thirty-nine figures given grim front-row seats to the earth's demise. *So long, Doc. If I'd seen this coming I'd have gotten you a better seat.* I shuddered as the faces of many of my own friends and comrades within the group flashed through my mind - but I forced the image as far back as I could.

The ACES pressure suits worn by the passengers were only good below 50,000 feet, but maliciously withstood the elements- or lack thereof- just long enough for the inevitable to descend upon their conscious with abject horror. Their last moments redefined cruelty. I shivered, speechless, and ran through a whirlwind of emotions before callous practicality further steeled my resolve. Our crew and those already onboard the station would last a whole lot longer with thirty-nine less mouths to feed. Seems Armageddon breeds a pretty cold bitch, no matter how you slice it.

The Commander stirred me from my philosophical reverie by calling for rendezvous procedures. I glanced to the external cameras and saw the gangly assemblage of the space station steadily approaching. About fifteen unmanned supply shuttles, each carrying more than 5,000 pounds of materiel, hovered in close, static, holding patterns around the station. They'd been launched around the clock since word of Halcyon broke.

Work crews looked like fat larvae clinging to the stations exterior performing the mother of all EVA's. They were doggedly affixing the boosters that would supposedly push the station beyond Halcyon's reach. Time truly was of the essence, and crews were affixing gossamer tethers to several of the supply shuttles, depressurization and docking procedures taking far too much time to execute now. Better to bring them along for the ride and unload them when safer space was reached.

Daylight faded once more to darkness below us, and the ominous visage of Halcyon loomed, close enough now to distinctly view its swirling surface, its impetus alone seeming to defy the very light of the sun. She was here. *So much for your figures, Doc. This party's getting crashed a little early.*

There was no escape. Lots and lots of space but zero time. We watched in stunned silence as the planet-sized object blotted out the stars, a death-star on steroids swallowing the vast horizon like some enormous, glowing iris exponentially expanding to infinity.

And then she stopped.

No massive blast of power, no tidal waves ripping across the planet's surface. Just a swirling gargantuan mass that... simply halted.

I blinked - I think - forced myself to take a breath. No one spoke. No one could.

The Commander pointed to a magnificent beam of white light radiating from Halcyon towards the heart of Australia, only for the briefest moment, then winking out. A corona plume of sparkling blue and white then began to emanate from the surface of Halcyon, a tentacle-like stream slowly spitting outward towards earth like some giant, accusatory finger. A slithering sausage as wide as Texas and lying squarely in our - and the space station's -direct orbital path.

The Commander gave me a quick look that spoke volumes. Fuel calculations were spinning through my brain and I gave him a quick nod, rapidly punching through the sequence to get the larger Orbital Maneuvering Systems (OMS) engines on-line. We had lots of gas, *Discovery* was supposed to help increase the station's altitude once we were docked, but no matter how we sliced it, this was gonna be close.

I relayed our course corrections to the station and counted off precious seconds as they updated their systems - forcing myself to keep my breathing under control, not wanting to convey my anxiousness across the open mike. "Alpha base, *Discovery* - stand by for course correction in ... 3, 2, 1 - firing."

The gray marble of earth above us shifted to the right as the Commander deftly coaxed *Discovery* on its new heading, well away from the quickly approaching finger. The station remained fixed off our starboard bow - a ballet of precision 300 miles above the earth at 17,000 mph.

Halcyon vanished from sight quicker than it came, sprinting off into space as we rolled into new morning above the rapidly flowing, gelatinous mass quickly spreading across the upper stratosphere - akin to some cosmic baker frosting a planetary cupcake. I stared incredulity directly in the eye and wondered with genuine concern if the Doctor's bottle of scotch was still in the cargo bay.

Here's to the luckiest friggin' co-pilot in the world...
Cheers, Doc.

Chapter One

Stirrings

I never found that bottle of Scotch.

A very decent thirty-year-old vintage of the Highland's finest single malt must still be circling the planet. Or maybe little, frozen Scotch-sicles now littered the surface of the stratosphere's new mystery skin. A terrible loss, one way or the other, and sorely missed.

"PERIWINKLES?" I stammered, "You hit the triple word score twice - 144 freakin" points! How am I supposed to follow THAT?"

"Next time, don't leave the word "wink"sitting between two triples. It's too much for a girl to resist."

Ninety-seven days and counting since Halcyon arrived and left. Ninety-seven days of gazing at a semi-translucent, rippling inferno of purplish color floating above the stratosphere with zero communication from the planet's surface - and the twenty-fifth day of my winless streak against the ever lovely, if overly astute, Major Elizabeth Hodgson, USAF. The chick was a walking dictionary. If Words with Friends® had been a gaming table in Vegas, she'd have bought the house with ease, smiling devilishly the whole time. I cursed the station's massive internal server and all the distractions it provided -Words included. What I wouldn't give for a lousy dart board. This chick would go down in some serious testosterone-fueled flames.

"Say it, Jarhead. A bet's a bet. Time to eat some crow," she cooed playfully, her auburn curls bouncing freely in the micro gravity. She must've washed her hair today.

I caught the lingering scent of perfumed shampoo - green apple, maybe? - glanced at my watch, then reached over and flipped the intercom switch to public address mode.

"Good morning, campers, and welcome to day 97 of year one 'Post Halcyon' - February 5th for you Terran-purist types. The time on deck is zero-eight-oh-one hours. Weather forecast looks promising - our temp today is 74.5 °F, one-tenth degree cooler than yesterday - so break out your mittens and parkas. Today is officially Dr. Wayne Dennis day, and our genius, resident-engineer-extraordinaire turns a youthful and exuberant 62. Please wish him well and thank him personally for the hillbilly music you'll be enjoying throughout the day.

"Operations reports no change in our status. All systems functioning in acceptable limits with one notable exception: please refrain from using the waste-collection station in lab two until the birthday boy has time to tone down the suction just a tad. You have been forewarned. All those suffering from painful and colorful butt-hickies will be publicly ridiculed incessantly by yours truly.

"In two hours, all personnel please report to the hangar for a special announcement from Colonel Garner and President Bielski. A little bird tells me there will be cake and some of the really good coffee from the President's own personal stash.

"At roughly noon our orbit will be directly over the eye and the boys and girls in Ops tell me we'll remain there for at least an hour and twenty-seven minutes. Our first long glimpse of the planet's surface through the galactic Saran Wrap in almost three weeks - so please plan accordingly. All personnel are reminded that communication scanning protocols are in effect throughout the day; all other work is secondary and should be shelved until we successfully traverse the eye." One gaping hole the size of the Mediterranean Sea afforded us a limited and occasional glimpse through the looking glass.

I paused briefly, a devilish little grin splaying across my face, then looked at Beth as if to ask 'anything else'? She shot me a playful and warning glare honed with a razor's edge, cooled only slightly by the playful twinkle in her rich, hazel eyes.

"... I almost forgot an important public service announcement, campers. This is, of course, your favorite resident naval aviator, Major Zacharias Absalom Dalton, United States Marine Corps, and being a man of impeccable integrity and unsullied honor, I must confess -under slight duress- that Dr. and Major Elizabeth Hodgson, U.S. Hair Force, is smarter, better looking and has a vocabulary that my simple Marine mind will never be able to match…"

I could hear scant laughter echoing through the station's corridors - more victims of Beth's vicious word-smithing, no doubt.

She smiled broadly and twirled her right hand in a 'keep-going' gesture.

"… and when we once again get the opportunity to fly through our own atmosphere, I've no doubt… well, maybe a little…"

Beth shot me a scathing look of barely veiled contempt.

"Okay… doubtless, and I repeat, doubtless… she is probably a better pilot, too - even though most chair force aviators drag their knuckles across the ground when they walk and don't have the luxury of knowing who their own parents were…."

I tried quickly floating beyond her reach, but Beth grabbed me and punched my upper arm - like Mike Tyson in a road rage incident - causing me to wince and guffaw over the loudspeaker, just as the station and shuttle Commander, Colonel Jim Garner, floated into the command module, grinning and shaking his head.

He neatly slipped my headset off as he drifted by, playfully shoving me into the bulkhead as I giggled and rubbed my tingling shoulder.

"Jim Garner here, folks - at this morning's meeting we'll also cast a vote deciding on whether or not to tar and feather our esteemed Marine and resident comedian. Division heads please report to command - Garner out."

Jim tossed the headset back to me and I switched the intercom to 'off'. I pulled up birthday boy Wayne's playlist on the command monitor and set it to random. Hank Locklin began twangily crooning his 1960 hit "Please Help Me I'm Falling in Love With You" over the station's internal speakers.

Beth looked sated and relatively happy - for once, and I reveled in her simple joy - a nice change from the morose gray clouding her disposition the last few weeks. Smiles were good. Any smiles. Her husband, Colonel Mark Hodgson, a great mentor and dear friend of mine, was one of those unfortunate souls Colonel Garner launched into space on the President's order as we left the planet. Beth and I had never spoke of it, but the animosity that hung between us the first few weeks on the station was pure, palpable tension. All of us had lost a lot of sleep wondering why President Bielski made that grim order, but officers don't question the Commander in Chief - at least to his face.

Beth and I had been friends for over a decade. The silly Words game was my own meager way of squirreling back into her somewhat good graces - but I knew in my heart of hearts she knew I could have - and probably - no, definitely- should have somehow intervened and prevented such a grave atrocity from ever happening. Lord knows the ghosts in my dreams said the same thing to me over and over, every night.

Beth and Mark had literally stood by my side four years ago when my wife Lisa succumbed to cancer - and I'd seemingly paid their friendship back by sitting idly by while her husband was launched into the vacuum of space. Beth refused to speak with the President at all and made a conscious effort to be as far away from him at all times as possible. If this meeting today didn't require all hands I knew for certain she'd find a way to ditch it. And probably still might.

Avoiding the President - and anyone else for that matter - was becoming much easier these days. Work crews had logged more hours in EVA's over the last ninety-seven days than NASA had accomplished in the previous ten years combined.

Seven prototype, inflatable modules developed by civilian corporations for the fledgling space-tourist industry had been steadily assembled and put into service around the station, affording more private quarters and a whole lot of breathing room for most of the station's forty residents. Four of the inflatables were accessible through crawl-ways, the three others primarily housing the worker crews accessible only by spacewalking. Beth had named them after the seven dwarves of Snow White fame. Sneezy, Bashful and Happy housed twenty-one crew-members and lazily rotated above the station; Sleepy, Dopey, Doc and Grumpy housed twelve people, positioned at four points along the station's frame. I still hung my hat in Discovery's crew bay. The remaining six crew, including Beth, were scattered in quarters throughout the station. Lots of elbow room, for sure.

"Let's go run, Zack. I've got the treadmills reserved for us at 8:30," Beth said, shooting off to the observation deck. She never looked at Jim, another casualty of her scorn. Although Beth was a career military officer and observed professional courtesies, I

13

could sense the discomfiture on Jim's face as she shot up past him through the hallway without so much as a peep.

"Hell hath no fury, right Zack?" whispered the Colonel.

"You got that right, skipper. You know how hard it's been for me to hold back and play dumb on Words for twenty-five days straight? Think I'm gonna quit takin' it easy on her from now on. I do think she's coming around, though."

Jim laughed and eyed me thoughtfully.

"You guys have always been close, Zack. And I'm afraid the President is about to put your relationship to the test even further."

I stared at him dumbly, awaiting a hint of what he alluded to, but soon realized he was going to remain tight-lipped.

"Am I going to like this?" I asked. "Or better yet, will she?"

Jim took a deep breath and looked at me long and hard.

"I think it beats the hell out of getting launched into space, Zack. That's all I'll say. The President will reveal all at the meeting."

I nodded, wondering what the ghosts of my dreams would say - even though I didn't have a clue as to what the President might have in store for us. I put a little more credence in the dreams. I started to head up the corridor when the Commander stopped me.

"Almost forgot this," he said, unzipping the cargo pocket of his flight suit and pulling out a king-size bag of peanut M&M's. "I know they're your favorite - found 'em stashed behind a monitor on Dopey last night. Who knows, this might very well be the last bag of M&M's in the world. Take 'em. I prefer the plain ones."

He floated them across to me and I quickly grasped the precious treasure with a bevy of mixed emotions. If he was giving me the last bag of M&M's in the world - whatever President Bielski had in store for us couldn't be that great. Ghosts be damned, though.

"Not pleased, Zack?"

I floated silently a moment then pocketed the candy.

"Very pleased, sir. Thanks a million. Really and truly great. Just wondering what this little taste of paradise is gonna cost me." An image of Professor Vandenberg batting away M&M's with a bottle of scotch like ping pong balls would no doubt haunt my dreams tonight.

Jim nodded in agreement and I went in pursuit of Beth,

knowing the next few hours would be both sweet and enlightening. Of the sweet I was certain, I could almost taste the chocolate, but somehow I knew the enlightenment may prove a tad more bittersweet.

Chapter Two
Revelations

Beth was pounding away mercilessly on the treadmill, her hair pulled back in a pony-tail that wavered to and fro like a windsock in a whirlwind. Her expression was placid and pensive beneath a thin sheen of perspiration, and I knew a million different wheels of logic and emotion were whirling through her mind. I knew it best not to interrupt her when she wore that expression.

"They're going to leave us, Zack," she stated casually, breathing smoothly and never letting up in her grueling pace. Jerry Reed belted out "East Bound and Down" in the background.

"I know." A lie, perhaps, or simply an acknowledgement to what my subconscious expected to hear during the President's briefing.

She turned and eyed me with a bemused grin, her ponytail arcing up and outward like a horse's tail caught flexing in mid-relief.

"Horse apples, Sherlock," she said, completing the horse imagery rather nicely I thought, and giggled.

"*...The boys are thirsty in Atlanta, and there's beer in Texarkana,*" crooned Jerry.

"Not entirely," I replied, tightly cinching down the straps that would allow me to generate a bit of resistance in the microgravity. I had yet to match Beth's grace on the machine, just one more feather in her cap of one-upmanship. She looked like a gazelle in full stride. I looked like I was scampering along in a full body cast with a broom handle shoved indelicately up my posterior. I loosened the straps connected to the harness around my waist just a tad and felt my gait even out - slightly, and with one more minor adjustment I loped into matching Beth's comfortable but challenging stride.

"You got to dodge and you got to duck it, you got to keep that diesel truckin', just put that hammer down and give 'er hell..."

"Other than Jim - you and I are the only remaining American military peeps on board," I offered in defense of my recent epiphany, "But I don't think they're really leaving us, per se. I think you and I may instead be leaving them." She eyed me curiously.

"Besides..." I added as our footfalls thrummed along in rhythm with a twangy electric guitar solo, "If they're leaving us - then where exactly might they be wandering off to? Last I checked the nearest Holiday Inn went out of business about 97 days ago." Beth said nothing and breathed deeply - then casually pointed a finger straight ahead towards the horizon. The moon was rising above the earth's curvature, a pale blue and silent witness to the shroud concealing its ancient neighbor. I wasn't certain if she simply wanted to point out the rising moon as a distraction or to say that that's where they were headed.

"...We've got a long way to go, and a short time to get there, I'm east bound, just watch ol' Bandit run."

We finished our workout in silence, sweating profusely and relishing the burn in muscles that longed for gravity's weighty embrace. Beth went to change into a fresh set of clothes and I told her I'd meet her at the shuttle in 15 minutes. She nodded an assent and threw her sweat-tinged towel in my face. More of that sweet, green-apple smell mixed with a hint of vinegar and jasmine filled my nostrils and I wiped my face dry, then Velcroed the towel to one of the observation rooms many air vents. The cool air chilled my skin slightly and I headed down the opposite corridor towards the shuttle and my berth.

I passed birthday boy Wayne in the corridor, presumably on his way to fix the lavatory, and wished him well in both efforts. He chuckled amiably, shaking his head and mumbling something about butt hickeys as I floated on by with a smile.

I thought about giving him the package of M&M's as a birthday gift, instead succumbing to greed and opted to keep them safely tucked away in my pocket, patting them gently just to hear that reassuring crinkle of canary-yellow paper rubbing against those colorful little orbs of delight. I'm a nice guy and all -

but come on - the *last* M&M's, *ever* - if I'd had two bags... no prob. But these babies were mine. Best I just keep these little goodies tucked away for a rainy day.

I crabbed my way on through the corridor and shot through the air lock to the main shuttle compartment. Kind of my own private corridor these days since the shuttle bay had been converted into 'the Hangar'. Basically, crews had installed a series of curved frames wrapped in thick insulation that spanned the cargo bay between the open cargo doors. It looked like a giant Conestoga wagon cover - the first-ever prairie schooner in space. The solar panels and coolant systems on the interior of the shuttle doors now provided more power to the station, while the open space made for a wonderful 'play room' for all the station's inhabitants, as well as an improvised movie theater.

Crew members could access the hangar via an airlock aft of the shuttle bay, leaving access to the cockpit primarily as my own exclusive domain. I was somewhat surprised to see President Bielski and one of the station's original Russian crew members - Lego-something - *Legoyavitch, that's it* - flipping through frequencies on the shuttles communication panel. Kind of a no-no in my book, and the look on both of their faces elevated my suspicions just a tad. My own face must have said so, too.

"Good morning, Zack" the President said, "Don't fret - we aren't taking her for a spin." Legoyavitch quickly said something in Russian over the mic, glanced to the President who made a swiping motion across his throat, then quickly toggled the comm panel off. The big Russian nodded casually and then brushed by me on his way up the air lock.

"What's up, sir?" I asked casually, moving towards my clothing locker to grab a fresh t-shirt.

"Just verifying some information before the meeting, Zack. The shuttle provides a little more privacy than some areas. I'm sure that's why you chose to hang your hat here." He smiled his million dollar grin, the same that helped him win two terms with ease, and I felt the hackles on the back of my neck rise slightly.

"It's not like she's my own private yacht, sir - I just don't get too many visitors, that's all. No disrespect intended, Mr. President."

He laughed amiably - another one of his polished political tools, no doubt. "Don't forget I was Air Force, Zack - way back in the day - I know what it feels like to have someone else pawing on 'my' gal." He tapped the console affectionately, smiled and then headed out the airlock. "See you at the briefing, Zack."

"With bells on, Mr. President." I stripped out of my flight suit, rank t-shirt and shorts, used some baby wipes to try and scrub away the worst of the funk on me, day-dreamed about a hot shower for the millionth time, when curiosity got the best of me. I floated naked across the cockpit, reactivated the comm panel the Russian had turned off and took note of the frequency he'd been using. We'd been scanning the whole gamut of military and civilian bands since we hit orbit - and this particular frequency was absolutely foreign to me. I plugged my headset into the comm panel, and just for giggles I toggled the mic three times - anyone listening on the other end would hear the staccato burst and might reply. After about five seconds a female voice said something unintelligible in Russian -along with one word I *did* know - Luna- and I quickly killed the comm panel, my heart racing.

I didn't speak Russian - other than a few bawdy toasts and some basic conversational stuff I'd picked up on my visits over the years to the Cosmodrome at Baikonur. But I *did* know everyone currently on board the station fairly well - and that didn't include any Russian-speaking females.

Whomever was on the other end of the line wasn't in the neighborhood, and for whatever reason, I felt that wasn't necessarily a good thing. I was pretty confident that 'Luna' in Russian meant exactly what I thought it meant. Involuntary chills crept across my naked body and I knew this was going to be one helluva briefing.

Chapter Three
Forty's A Crowd

Doctor 'Mouse' Timmons was the first to arrive, clutching his iPad close to his chest and sporting a huge grin. Of all the geniuses on board, in spite of his rather diminutive stature, this guy stood head and shoulders above the rest. Dude had graduated from MIT when he was fourteen with multiple advanced degrees in areas I couldn't even spell, let alone comprehend. But unlike many prodigies, he still possessed a modicum of social skills, and he and I had become fast friends. Humor seemed a rather elusive concept for many of the elite geek-set — at least my brand of humor, anyways — but Mouse always laughed at my jokes, even the lame ones, which made him alright in my book.

"You have got to check this out, Zack!" he said excitedly, lobbing the iPad across the cockpit like a frisbee. I snatched it out of the air as he brushed past me, sliding gracefully into the Commander's seat, his usual perch when we were hanging out and watching Earth spin below us.

"You didn't take any more naked pictures of the first lady, did you?" I said. Mouse was perpetually snapping photos - mostly of the planet's surface, trying to make sense of the mystery skin shrouding the planet, but occasionally getting some images that ruffled the rest of the crew's feathers. In another life the sandy-haired 25-year old could've been paparazzi, no doubt.

"Way better than that, Zack. Just look, man."

I activated the iPad and the familiar image of the purple skin covering earth popped up in crisp, high definition.

"Nice pic, Mouse - but I've got the real thing right there in front of me."

"Look closer, man. See anything peculiar?"

I scoured the image, but all I could see were the familiar whirls and swirls I'd gleaned over the last three months, peppered with the occasional dark spots and squiggly lines that looked like erratic veins or rivers skimming across the atmosphere at 60,000 feet.

I held the iPad where he could also look at the image. "Sorry, Mouse - I don't see anything different."

"My bad," he said. "Go to the next image."

I flipped to the next picture in the library - and something that *was* very different immediately popped into view.

The landscape was still a vibrant purple, sort of like looking at the moon through a bottle of Welch's Grape soda, but the distinct outline of a perfect, silver sphere blocked out a large section of the center of the photo.

"What the hell is that?" I asked, zooming in to get a closer glimpse of the silver-dollar sized object. Mouse was grinning like he'd just pulled off the perfect prank as the image adjusted itself on the screen.

The object was a dull silver, definitely metallic, with eight trapezoid-shaped darker areas radiating from the center. Textbook flying saucer stuff, right out of a 1950's era movie, and absolutely enormous. The sun cast a shadow from the object across the surface of the 'sky-skin', the moniker most of the crew had given the grand, purple haze draping the planet. This thing was bigger than Dallas, if my quick guesstimations were right.

"You messing with me?" I asked.

He continued to grin and shook his head quickly from side-to-side. If anything, Mouse was a bit too chipper, and brazenly honest - the one guy on the station that seemed unflappable, even in the face of Armageddon.

"No, man. I took this about an hour ago - no shit. I haven't even shown the commander or anyone in Ops. Whaddya think it is?"

"Dude - it's a freakin' flying saucer - unless you've been playing around in photoshop."

I scanned his face for any signs of deception, but the same perpetual, boyish grin was all I could see.

After Halcyon had arrived, any misconceptions I'd had about life elsewhere in the universe had naturally vanished - but this was still unnerving.

"You think these are the ones that laid down the sky-skin?" I asked.

Mouse had always been vocal in professing his beliefs with me about UFO's. I now knew more about every crazy conspiracy theory that had ever been tossed around before Halcyon showed up than I cared to admit. If he hadn't been a genius way off the scales it would have undoubtedly prevented him from working with the space program. But NASA tolerated his quirks - a lot of the systems on the space station attesting to the guy's genius, and their tolerance.

"Somebody's checking it out, Zack - I wonder if this has anything to do with what the President is going to say?"

Voices began to filter in from the cargo bay as the personnel arrived for the briefing.

"Let's go get some of that cake and find out."

****

Beth was the last to arrive - no surprise, and she joined Mouse and I near the airlock forward of the cargo bay. The rest of the crew were stationed around the perimeter of the bay, munching on the promised cake, and President Bielski stood center-stage, hooking his stockinged feet into the velcro straps on the floor.

Mouse was trying to show Beth the picture of the UFO, but she stood with her arms crossed, wearing a grim expression and thoroughly ignoring him.

"Good morning, people," the President said, "I'll keep this as brief as possible. We've got a lot of work to do in the next couple of days and I'd like for us to get started as soon as possible. In a nutshell - we are leaving."

Murmurs around the room echoed off the walls, and Beth shot me a scathing "I told you so" look. I just shrugged my shoulders and focused intently on the President, who was motioning for the crowd to get silent.

"I've been reviewing archival information the last few weeks that had somehow been classified beyond my own purview prior to Halcyon's arrival. Unbeknownst to me and everyone else in government, it seems that we have a base on the moon that was created jointly with the Russians - and others- back in the early 60's. The facility is self-supporting and has been manned with a small but permanent crew for almost 50 years."

The President let that statement sink in, and the murmurs transformed into a hushed and somber silence.

"No doubt the arrival of Halcyon transformed all of our belief structures, we are apparently not alone in the universe, and the documents and images I've been reviewing the last few days have strained my own beliefs to the breaking point, to say the least. Dim the lights, would you, Wayne?"

The engineer stood by a control panel midway in the cargo bay, where all the lighting and audio visual controls were housed. A projector suspended midway in the hangar hummed to life, and an image of former President Eisenhower lit up the screen in the rear of the cargo bay. Mouse gigged me in the ribs with his elbow, his eyes wide.

"Dr. Timmons will no doubt tell you all about what most of us considered to be ludicrous fantasy just a few short months ago. Turns out he and all the other UFO nuts weren't wrong. According to what I've been reading, in 1955 Eisenhower met with an alien race and established a treaty at Edwards Air Force base. That treaty resulted in the construction of a lunar base, among other things, and also a loose alliance with the aliens most of us know from popular fiction as the Greys or Zeta Reticulans."

The President began displaying different slides. Images of the Greys, various spacecraft, and what was undoubtedly the current lunar facilities flashing across the screen. Mouse was awestruck, his mouth wide open. Beth still looked pissed and unmoved. What the hell did she know that I didn't?

"For some reason," the President continued, "information about this relationship has been kept from the public in a huge way, and I have no answers as to why. Whomever decided to shroud this info apparently never anticipated Halcyon, and even more shocking to me, neither did the Greys. Whatever secret, shadow government that embraced this veil of secrecy perished in the last conflagration, and we may never know why all of this occurred as it did...." The President's voice quavered, rare for a man that seemed to always have an answer for anything.

"...But that doesn't change what we need to do now to ensure the survival of our species. In the next few days, the seven dwarves will be tethered together and affixed with the engines Dr. Timmons designed, and we will head to the moon." The President fixed me with a hard stare.

"Not all of us will be making the journey, though. It's imperative that someone remain here and monitor the sky-skin up close, and hold out for the possibility of communicating with survivors on the surface. I know not all of you are Americans, and I think the concept of borders died when that shroud covered our planet. My last official order as President of the United States and Commander-in-Chief is to place Majors Dalton and Hodgson here as observers - and I will allow anyone else who chooses so to remain here with them."

Every eye in the room looked at us with pity as Wayne turned the lights up to normal. I was stunned and said with confidence the only thing a Marine could when given a direct order.

"Aye, aye, sir."

Chapter Four

Contact

Over the next 48 hours, Mouse became the big man on campus. If crews weren't working on transferring provisions and prepping the dwarves for transit, they were hanging out in the hangar listening to Mouse preach about the aliens and what he knew. It was hilarious to hear prominent scientists who'd once scoffed at UFO buffs asking questions about Nordic aliens and ascension to different dimensions. Mouse was digging it. The dude was in his element.

Beth wasn't.

I hadn't seen her for more than five minutes since the President gave us our orders. She'd simply said "Yes, sir" and shot out of the cargo bay without even looking at me. Not exactly a promising start for the person I was likely to spend the rest of my days with. Colonel Garner told me she was working on our provisions and resources, and in the mean time I set up the communications protocol with Luna base, and oh yeah... I met my first aliens.

Turns out the female Russian I'd thought I hung up on wasn't Russian at all. She was an Australian scientist and linguist named Christina Franks, who'd been stationed at Luna base for 10 years... working with freaking aliens! Once we knew the comm frequencies to Luna, Mouse set up a video link in Ops, and I had the most bizarre briefing of my entire adult life. Beth even came out of hiding to sit in on it, but her body language told me it was only because she had to. I couldn't understand why this upset her as much as it did, but I figured we had plenty of time ahead of us to sort it out.

Colonel Garner, President Bielski and Mouse hovered behind Beth and I in Operations as the monitors to Luna base flickered to life, revealing Dr. Franks standing in the center of what I presumed to be Luna's own operations center. Banks of monitors and stations appeared to her left and right in a broad semicircle, manned by three people - and one of the Greys. I heard Mouse let out a tiny, awestruck giggle. I was completely dumbfounded, and apparently so were the rest of us.

Dr. Franks began laughing. "Forgive my saying so, but you should really see the look on your faces right now - absolutely priceless!" She had a warm and inviting smile, instantly likable. 'Priceless' sounded more like 'proisless', no mistaking her thick, Aussie tongue. She pushed back an errant curl of fiery red hair into a mane of crimson curls that cascaded beyond her shoulders in waves, affording us a better glimpse of very-green eyes above lightly freckled cheeks. "Some of our residents do take some getting used to, I'm afraid, but I assure you the shock will eventually pass." The other people monitoring the banks, and the alien, joined Dr. Franks in the center of the room with steps more akin to gliding than walking. It appeared there was some gravity on the station, but much lighter than Earth-normal. Looked like it might take some getting used to.

"I'm Christina Franks, I run the communications division. To my right is our resident Brit, Dr. Colin Peters, head of research and to my left are Doctors Blake and Shelley Hanks, who oversee our medical facilities." Each of those introduced gave a nod and a kind wave. "...And this is Balthus of Zeta Reticuli, a permanent consultant, if you will, and liaison between us and other species. He doesn't say much. Director Salek will be joining us in just a few moments." The alien Balthus raised a three-fingered right hand, glanced at those he was with, then returned to a station whose purpose eluded me.

"So that was first contact," I mumbled. "Kind of thought it would be a bigger deal."

Christina laughed. "I assure you, sir. It gets better."

From a corridor behind her a very tall humanoid emerged, towering at least two feet above the rest of the group.

"Forgive my tardiness, Mr. President. I've been overseeing the preparations for your group's arrival. I'm the director of this facility, please call me Salek." Salek was fair complected, with a tousle of sandy blonde hair that reminded me of a frontman for some 80's metal, hair-band. He had enormous, almond-shaped, oversized eyes of a deep turquoise, and what I can only describe as delicate features hung on an impressive and imposing frame. Kind of like a trimmer, albino version of Shaq - with David Bowie hair and a full, resonant voice that demanded attention, but conveyed a honeyed warmth.

The President introduced each of us, then fell silent - shocked to speechlessness.

"I know you all have many questions - and all will be answered in due time. Suffice it to say that right now, we need you as much as you need us. I hope you believe me when I say we were supposed to meet on entirely different circumstances, but fate seems to have a cruel sense of humor."

"The vessel you called 'Halcyon' is manned by a species foreign to even us; their technology and the presence of the so-called sky-skin they left over Earth has had a dampening effect on our own propulsion and other systems from the moment they were first discovered entering the solar system. Our vessels have been unable to leave the moon's orbit and were unable to intervene as planned during the global crisis; mankind failed itself - but we also failed in the role we were supposed to play, and for that I must apologize..."

"...And to answer the question that's on all of your minds, I am part human and what you call 'alien' - a hybrid. I was born here on this station, and you may not completely understand this yet, but I've also been the sole director of this facility since its inception. You'll understand better in the next few days, I assure you. I will leave you in the capable hands of Christina, who will work out the logistics of the next few days. It was an honor and privilege meeting all of you."

"And you, Director Salek," the President said. "Forgive me for being taken aback. This is quite the shock, and I, too, wish it were under different circumstances. I hope we can be of a great benefit and service to one another, and I look forward to meeting you face-to-face."

President Bielski and Colonel Garner left Ops to continue overseeing movement preparation, leaving Mouse, Beth and I to lay the groundwork for other things to come.

If all went according to plan, the dwarves would fly tethered to the moon powered by the ion engines designed by Mouse specifically for these vessels. They were originally designed to be space ferries, taking rich space tourists on a ten day cruise to the moon and back. Looked like this was gonna be more of a one-way trip for most of them, but not all.

Mouse would spend a few days on Luna Base getting up to speed on their systems, then return with Christina, Colin — and Balthar to upgrade our observation equipment and see what we could learn about the sky-skin and the source of the trans-dimensional radiation dampening the alien technologies. The Dwarves would serve as supply vessels to keep us replenished from the ample lunar stores, and as shuttles for the eventual transfer of personnel somewhere down the road.

I don't think I've ever needed a drink more than when we finally finished that call. All those conversations about E.T. I'd had with Mouse came flooding back, and I wish I'd paid closer attention. One little tidbit I hadn't forgotten, though. In all of Mouse's stories, the Zeta Reticulans were supposed to be the bad guys, the chief culprits in the whole abduction scenario, and now one of them was apparently moving in.

There goes the neighborhood.

Chapter Five
Cabin Fever

Colonel Jim Garner granted my wish later that evening, joining Mouse and I in the hangar and toting a large, plastic, drinking-sleeve filled with the smoothest Kentucky bourbon you've ever sucked through a straw. After passing the bag a few times, I got on the intercom and requested that Beth join us. She actually showed up a few minutes later and took a long pull on the bag before I could even offer it to her, and then started laughing hysterically.

For a minute I thought she'd gone off the deep end, but the bourbon loosened my resolve and I started laughing right along with her. Mouse and Jim soon following suit. I still don't know why we did, but felt a hell of a lot better afterwards, and the bag passed between us freely and frequently over the next few hours as we reflected on everything and anything - except for the present and all that it threatened or promised.

The booze hit the Colonel pretty hard and he passed out midway while telling us about a fishing trip he took with Neil Armstrong and Gordon Cooper. One minute he was laughing hard, the next he was sawing logs, so Mouse and I wrapped him in a blanket and velcro-ed him to the ceiling. I hadn't seen Jim laugh that hard since we were back on earth - Lord knows the guy needed a serious dose of de-stressor, hell, we all did.

I patted the Colonel on the face and attempted to say "Sweet dreams, sir", but it came out more like "Schweet dreamssir." Damn good bourbon. Been awhile, I reckon.

Drinking in zero-g is kind of trippy. Literally. You know that woozy feeling you get when just one too many slips over the gums and the world starts to get that little lean and sway to it? Take that woozy wave, free it from gravity's bounds and you're setting smooth sail aboard the S.S. Bourbon to HappyTown. I decided then and there that Mouse needed to build a moonshine still - and soon.

Beth decided we all should do some yoga, and shot down my suggested game of 'who-can-spit-in-this-bucket-across-the-cargo-bay'; Mouse said he was content just drifting and gabbing. Apparently Mouse won.

"Spin me, Zack - but not too fast or I'll hurl." Mouse said, floating my way.

I hooked my foot into a strap on the cargo floor and Mouse twisted into a fetal position, hands wrapped tight around his shins, face tucked close to his knees. We'd done this a lot -plenty of time on our hands - and had just about perfected it. I put my left hand on the scruff of his skinny neck, the other grasping his ankles, then corkscrewed him like I was starting the engine on a vintage biplane - but with more finesse, and perhaps a bit more force than he asked for. Okay, a lot more.

Mouse was spinning like a pinwheel in a hurricane and just barely floating into the center of the cargo bay. This one would be a new record. I heard him mumble 'asshole' as he slowly began extending his arms and legs - eyes squeezed shut - hell, I thought I was gonna puke just watching him twirl, but his face remained placid and no chunks were redecorating the hangar.

"A mouse in motion tends to stay in motion," quipped Beth, stretching into an elegant crescent moon pose.

I stretched my arms out and clasped my hands behind my head, afloat on a calm and peaceful river of bourbon bliss.

"Mouse, I'm wondering about something the President said this morning in the briefing. You never told me you'd talked to him about the UFO stuff," I said, drifting along on my lazy river.

"He started asking me about it last month, after he had me hack into one of the laptops we recovered from the shuttle. I'm guessing it was the archive info with the details on Luna Base. One of the passengers that didn't make it on board must have been a part of the program..."

"Didn't make it on board?!" Beth roared. "They were launched into space and murdered on his orders, Mouse! And we had enough stores and space to accommodate every last one of them - you know that better than anyone."

"I'm so sorry, Beth... I wasn't thinking... please forgive me - it's the bourbon, and the spinning..."

"Shut up, Mouse." I said. "You need to get this out, Beth, and I figure now is as good a time as any - this has been a long time coming. Mouse didn't have a damn thing to do with what happened, and you know it."

Anger and tears brimmed in her eyes and I thought she was gonna bolt but I stared her down hard, liquid courage fueling my resolve. "If you want to blame somebody - you blame me. Mark was my best friend, Beth!"

She took a few deep breaths, forcing herself to calm down, then eyed me severely.

"Zack, you don't get it. This isn't about blame. The President's a liar and guilty as hell, and no matter what you think, I don't blame you or that snoring cocoon up there for what happened. Do I think you could and should have disobeyed that order, YES! But that doesn't change the 'why', Zack. Bielski wanted somebody on that shuttle dead, and it's all because of Luna Base... that was Mark's laptop, Zack. He was part of the Luna project." She put her face in her hands, crying softly.

Mouse had stopped spinning and sat staring open-mouthed at Beth, then looked at me for answers.

I didn't have any. Just a thousand questions.

"Come on, Beth - that's crazy - if Mark had been in any way associated with this stuff I would've known about it - we were practically glued to each other's hips over the last decade. I don't buy it."

She daubed her eyes with her sleeve and took a deep, shuddering breath.

"He never knew that I knew. Nobody did. And I plan on keeping it that way. At least I did."

"How did you know?" I asked, still not wanting to fully believe her, Mouse nodding in silent agreement.

She eyed us both carefully, then proceeded to tell us a story that just about ruined a perfectly good drunk. Almost, but not quite.

If anything, it was a damn good way to send off Mouse and Jim - and highly enlightening.

Things were about to get truly interesting around here.

Chapter Six

Voyages

Beth manned operations inside the station while I finished up my external, visual inspection of Sleepy, the last in the convoy bound for the moon. I disconnected the tether holding me to the floating condo, and pushed gently away. I'd been in the suit for almost six hours and was ready to get back inside the station, but I wanted a good view of the launch, and this was the best spot for that. Another few minutes wouldn't kill me.

"Gravy train, you are good to go for Luna Base. I'm clear. Let 'er rip, Colonel - and Godspeed. And don't forget my moon-rock, Mouse. See you in a few weeks."

"About damn time, " said Jim over the scratchy comm-link, "Service around this place sucks. You take care of each other and keep your eyes on that sky-skin. Learn what you can, boys and girls. And play nice. Gravy train commencing launch sequence, - firing in 3, 2, 1… launch."

The pylon-mounted ion engines on the Dwarves pulsed into life simultaneously and the convoy slowly snaked off into the deep, the computers gradually adjusting thrust and attitude on each vessel until the tethers became taut and the convoy moved forward as one. Liquid fueled boosters bloomed into life, and the floating subdivision quickly faded from view. Quite the show. Wish I had popcorn.

I soaked up the majesty around me, noting how much smaller the station appeared with the Dwarves gone. I tried to spot them in the void, but they had already gone way beyond my vision… but something else was out there, of that I no longer had any doubts.

I flew the jet-pack back to the airlock, looking like a pink marshmallow floating against the black of space, lit up by the purple glare of the sky-skin. Thirty minutes later I was happily relieving myself and contemplating a long nap, but Beth and I had a lot to talk about, and a lot of work to do.

She'd put some light classical music on over the PA, then joined me in the dining area for our first dinner together as sole occupants of the ISS. I grabbed two meals at random from the storage rack and threw them in the 'oven', then sipped on a pouch of coke, floating another to her.

"Thanks," she said, "What's for dinner, roomie?"

"I left it to the tangled twists of fate, I fear. Whatever the universe has in store." The oven timer chimed, and I pulled out the individual platters, sticking them to the table top.

Beth peeled back the foil top, revealing a shrimp gumbo over rice - one of the better meals, and I unwrapped a Salisbury steak. Fourth night in a freaking row, and unfortunately, *not* one of the better ones.

"Seems your universal path has something to do with cows," she said, digging into her gumbo and slurping up an errant grain of rice trying to escape her jaws.

She'd lightened up considerably since her confession to Mouse and I. Even going so far as to give Jim a big hug before he boarded the convoy. Sharing her burden seemed to change everything, although the news had soured my attitude a bit. I still had a lot to sort through before I could make any decisions, one way or another.

I trusted Beth.

And I believed her.

But the stuff she was talking about was bat-shit crazy, and I still couldn't wrap my head around it. The rational part of my mind still wanted more proof. Sure, I'd now seen aliens and there was a global, purple saran wrap outside my window - but now the person I'd been assigned to a life-long post with was claiming to play a role in the bigger scheme of things.

Beth told Mouse and I that she'd been in constant contact with an alien race since she was four years old.

And we were the first people she'd ever told. Not even her husband Mark knew.

And yet they still gave her a security clearance? How the hell could she keep something that bizarre a secret?

33

She told us the spaceship Mouse had photographed was 'her' aliens, trying to project outside of the sky-skin just long enough to communicate with her. They were trapped on the planet just like those at Luna Base, and could only emerge beyond the skin for seconds before the radiation folded them back into their previous space. Beth's aliens were supposedly the good guys, and it was that determination I was struggling with; it bugged me to no end, but not half as bad as her belief that we were supposed to destroy the station and return to earth in the next couple days - that one was kind of a biggie.

"How long before we get to the eye and you ...we... 'talk' with them?" I asked.

"About twenty minutes. You sure you're up for this?" She looked genuinely concerned, no doubt due to the lack of confidence my eyes conveyed.

"Beth - lets get this phone call between us and E.T. out of the way - then I might have a better feeling about what you've told me. Fair enough?"

She nodded, sipping the last of her coke. Her face conveyed a simple vulnerability - and perhaps a little bit of trust? It was a huge leap of faith for her to clue Mouse and I in on her 'experiences' - and I somehow wished she hadn't. I liked my world the way it was before aliens entered the picture. I'd dreamed about meeting extraterrestrials as a kid, but there is something to be said about getting what you wish for.

I ate the last of my Salisbury steak and stabbed my fork into the reconstituted mashed potatoes and gravy. I really did like the gravy, but four days of it kind of dampened what little appetite I had left.

"Let's get this over with, Beth - but you might want to change the music. Maybe the soundtrack from *Close Encounters of the Third Kind* would be more apropos." I smiled as best as I could, and relief seemed to paint her complexion with a rosy glow.

"You cooked - I'll do the dishes," she said, peeling the trays from the table and scraping the leftover foodstuffs into a container for mulching in the arboretum, a task that was harder to accomplish than you think. It took a deft hand not to scatter food all over the galley and send green beans off on little quests throughout the station. It was always rather unpleasant to be drifting down a corridor and get smacked in the face with stray food, but it happened more often than not. *One plus of having fewer mouths to feed on the station.*

We floated our way up to Ops, and I felt an overwhelming sense of aloneness. Space is deathly quiet, and now with everyone heading off to Luna Base, the silence seemed deafening. I don't think I'd felt that alone since my wife passed away. A memory of sitting alone and sipping the last of her favorite wine while I stared at the walls came rushing to mind unbidden, and I had to fight back despondency with both fists. *This ain't the time to be melancholy,* I thought and wiped away an errant tear that somehow made its way past my resolve. *Suck it up, Marine - time to talk to E.T.*

Beth was floating near the observation window, her face pressed close to the glass. The eye through the sky-skin loomed just ahead.

"Okay," she breathed. "We need to get started. I have to relax completely - and so do you. You'll need to hold my hands and quiet your mind in order to hear Lothar speak. I've been doing this my whole life and it's still a bit disconcerting at times. Just don't let fear or discomfort addle you; this is simply a new way of communicating, Zack."

I took a few deep breaths and futilely tried to calm myself - until Beth grabbed both my hands. That simple human connection made me breathe a little easier, and my heart-rate began to slow. She began the process of lulling me into a near-hypnotic state of deep relaxation. Her voice was soothing, liquid valium and I easily succumbed in spite of my apprehension.

Little did I know that in the next five minutes life as I knew it would never be the same.

Chapter Seven
Clear As Mud

It's kind of difficult to explain what it was like to hear Lothar's voice in my mind for the first time. Back on earth I'd gone to a wealthy friend's home after he'd finished installing a new, private, home-theater... sub-woofers built into the seats, a gazillion speakers all around the room - a truly immersive, cinematic experience - yet it paled in comparison to the resonance and vibrations during this 'link' with Lothar and Beth. I was proud of myself for not totally freaking out.

Lothar 'told' me that he was of the alien species known as Orions. I say 'told' because I can't think of a better way to describe the images, emotions and knowledge conveyed to me within the simultaneous barrage of data. It wasn't like Lothar was just a voice in my head - more like Lothar's entire soul was jacked into mine - along with Beth's. All their feelings, emotions, memories - conveyed to me in gentle, overwhelming waves. It took me a few minutes to really process all that was happening, and it wasn't until I mentally 'let go' that the messages became cogent and clear. And let me tell you, it was a helluva message.

Lothar sounded like Tom Selleck on helium. A resonant bass timbre offset by a child-like pitch of soothing tones. The sincerity conveyed in his speech and presence was staggering, like one of those chance encounters with someone you instantly bond with. Any doubts I'd had about Beth's veracity were quelled - although I adamantly refused to blow up the station, and Lothar calmly acquiesced to my plea. Mouse and the others would still need a home whenever they returned from Luna Base, and I was not about to destroy the last vestige of humanity's reach to the heavens.

In the half-hour we traversed the eye, I learned more than I ever did in high school, Annapolis and grad school combined. It wasn't as if I'd received some kind of massive download- you might call it that, somewhat - but there were a lot of unspoken questions I received answers to, and I had a greater appreciation of our situation. Still wasn't too sure about how to rightfully proceed - but I knew more than when I woke up this morning. Doubt may have been erased - but suspicion wasn't vanquished entirely.

The Orions seemed to be just as puzzled by Halcyon as the 'other' aliens at Luna Base. Lothar kept repeating over and over, "there are those that we are greater than, and there are those far greater than us... we are studying."

Lothar also told us that those on Luna Base were deceivers - but not all of them. Director Salek was who he purported to be, but the Zeta Reticulan known as Balthus was not. Balthus was actually of a Reptilian species - a highly advanced, cruel race bent on enslaving mankind known as the Drakos. The Drakos had the ability to make humans and other races perceive them in any way they wanted to - and in Balthus' case, he had everyone believing that he was of the Zeta Reticulan species - the Grey's to most humans. With some difficulty, Lothar and other Orions were able to see past the Reptilian guise, but their efforts over the years to convey this information to Director Salek had been thwarted repeatedly. With the arrival of Halcyon and the placement of the sky-skin, those efforts had been further hampered, but Lothar seemed to believe that all was not yet lost.

I learned that prior to Halcyon's arrival humanity had been teetering on the verge of a grand transformation. A step forward in evolution that hinged simply upon humanity's belief that we were not alone in the universe. Roughly 35% of the planet's population had believed in life elsewhere, with that figure shooting up to 45% when news of Halcyon broke. Lothar said the magic number was 50% - and if we had achieved that level of belief world-wide then the grim armageddon that played out would never have occurred. It would've basically flipped a big evolutionary switch and allowed humanity to move on to its next level.

Lothar projected imagery from an alternate time-line, showing me what life on earth would have been like had the shift occurred. The beauty of it had brought me to tears - and the knowledge that we were so close to moving beyond our simple existence saddened me deeply. So close yet so freaking far.

But all was not yet lost, supposedly.

Lothar said that there were still pockets of humanity littered around the globe. The sky-skin seemed to nullify and absorb radiation in a way that perplexed even the Orions, and within just a few day's time, save for a few heavily hit areas, the earth would once again be habitable; albeit much darker. The physical devastation from the nuclear weapons could not be undone, but the lingering effects of lethal radiation were almost completely eradicated. Many on the planet would still succumb to exposure to lethal doses of radiation, but others would get past it - and eventually flourish again. Lothar estimated the planet's eventual population to level out at about 13 million. We'd blasted ourselves back to a population that hadn't existed since the dawn of agriculture tens of thousands of years ago. Earth was now a purple-hued gravesite for more than 5 billion souls vanquished in a matter of hours. How could we have been so foolish when opportunity for better things was so damn close? And why the hell didn't we know about this?!

As the connection faded with Lothar I looked at Beth, blinking away frustrating tears and swooning from the emotional connection I'd just experienced. She looked guilty and ashamed, and the lingering effects of the link carried her emotional despondency to me in a trickling flow of pain. Her hands still rested in mine, and I gave her a gentle squeeze then wiped the errant tear drops from my face. When I broke the connection, I still felt a tendril of something linking us, and I could sense her deep guilt. She blamed herself for the downfall of man - and she knew I knew it. The weight of so much loss borne upon her shoulders -unnecessarily- definitely explained her behavior over the past few months, but I was still at a loss in trying to determine how to comfort her.

I think she understood my inability to say anything, the softness in her eyes and a feeble, gentle smile the only communication between us as I drifted off down the corridor to the safety of my cubby hole in the shuttle - with more on my mind than I could possibly comprehend.

Chapter Eight
Luna Calling

The next few days Beth and I didn't talk much. There wasn't any animosity - I just think I needed some time to process through all the information I'd garnered from Lothar. There was a lingering effect of the link, or just willful imagining on my part - not too sure either way; I swear I could hear Beth's thoughts on occasion, and the sideways glances she gave me when we were doing our routine work in Ops told me that she was hearing me, too.

I was lazily floating around the hangar, reading through some of the UFO stuff Mouse had given me while sipping on a little bourbon Jim had left, when the familiar strains of 'Thus spake Zarathustra' began chiming from my I-Pad - Mouse was calling on the secure link he'd embedded into our systems.

"Greetings from Luna Base, Zack! This place is cool as hell, man!"

Mouse's sandy-brown locks bounced around his grinning face - guess he finally got the chance to meet the ET's he'd been dreaming about his whole life. His expression was the epitome of stunned pride and elation.

"Are the Twinkies still in the fridge?" I asked - using our pre-arranged code to determine if others were listening.

"Twinkies are chilling, Zack - all is cool."

I floated towards one of the comm panels to summon Beth, but she floated into the cargo bay before I could hit the switch... I swear she could read my thoughts.

She smiled at Mouse and took a long pull on the bourbon-bag, and we both repeated to Mouse what we'd discovered from our session with Lothar.

Mouse was surprisingly cool with the new information. I guess years of speculation and wonder about fringe elements made swallowing this new information as easy as pie. We agreed to keep the information strictly between ourselves - no need to trouble Jim, the President or anyone else until we were able to learn more.

Mouse was obviously distracted by a newfound obsession with Dr. Christina Franks, Luna Base's communication specialist. He mentioned the vivacious, redheaded Aussie's name about half a dozen times in the space of a few minutes. If a face ever truly conveyed 'whipped' - it was Mouse's.

While Mouse was still on the line, klaxons and flashing lights began pealing through the station. This meant only one thing - we'd been breached by something. Beth and I instinctively went into emergency mode, leaving the hangar as quick as possible for the nearest Soyuz capsule. Tiny asteroids no bigger than a pebble were shredding through the hangar as we fled, a fusillade of lethal, jagged daggers. One of them punched straight through the fleshy part of my neck, leaving a wicked gash as I dove through the escape pod's hatch, Beth right behind me.

The Soyuz hull was pinging like a thousand, steel, ball-bearings dancing in a dryer as hundreds of the tiny asteroids peppered its exterior. I dogged the hatch closed and Beth began wrapping a bandage around my bleeding neck. Sounds of shredding fabric and escaping oxygen reverberated through the hull as Beth and I clambered into the waiting pressure suits, praying the link to Ops hadn't been severed yet. My hands were flying over the controls as the sounds of devastation continued to unravel around us.

The Soyuz received the location of the eye in the sky-skin moments before the link was broken. The primary systems in Ops must have succumbed to the barrage. I backed the Soyuz away from the airlock blindly, and within only 15 feet the barrage on the outer hull subsided. I banked the module and Beth and I crowded around the single porthole to get a glimpse of the damage to the station.

It was totaled. The whole of the ISS looked like it had been sprayed with a thousand machine guns. Oxygen vented into space from every section, debris floating into the vacuum from a few jagged, gaping holes you could drive a Buick through.

Beth jumped on the comm and began broadcasting a mayday

to Luna Base as I programmed our reentry.

"I hear Montana's nice this time of year - how's that sound to you?" I asked.

"Beats the hell out of being right here, Zack. Let's go."

I took one last look out the porthole - too shocked to really process everything, then engaged the reentry systems.

I guess Lothar finally got what he wanted after all.

Chapter Nine
Home

Beth and I were strapped in tight for the reentry. The first bumps of the atmosphere greeted us with a vibrating jolt as we slipped through the eye of the sky-skin, a scant magenta light seeping in through the lone porthole; bathing the cabin in garish and smoky stage light like the front row of a Deep Purple concert. I prayed the sturdy Russian craft hadn't taken too hard of a drumming from the meteor shower, but if the shielding failed I wouldn't even have time to cuss before we cooked like a marshmallow absently dropped in a campfire…

"Pitch is a tad steep, Zack" cautioned Beth, a scant second before I began adjusting our descent. The Soyuz was shaking like a '57 Greyhound bus with bad shocks going a hundred miles an hour down a gravel road — and seemed to be about as responsive as one of the old cruisers. My minor course and pitch corrections were doing little to alleviate the jolting, and the vessel creaked and popped like a submarine plunging swiftly beyond its crush depth.

The first tendrils of gravity started digging their fingers into our chests as the purple atmosphere roared a welcome all around us, a brisk and violent 'hello' as we plunged to earth at almost 800 feet per second - about fifty feet a second too fast. Warning lights were flashing across the control panel and I hoped the drogue chute could handle the extra strain. I raised the pitch a tad more and watched the air-speed bleed off back into a more acceptable rate just as the drogue chute deployed, and was greeted by the welcome 'thud' of the four main drop-chutes deploying. Gravity punched a hole square in my gut - a hit that never felt so good. Terra Firma in eight more minutes.

The braking engines fired when sensors detected the ground's steady approach and the Soyuz landed with a mumbled thump that rocked us both pretty hard, but the craft remained upright. We sat there in the quiet as I shut down the main systems, the Soyuz still hissing and popping as its hull cooled from reentry. The whole cabin was dimly lit by the purple twilight streaming through the porthole. I unlatched and removed my helmet and leaned back in the seat, sucking wind hard. Gravity was welcome, but it pressed down on places untouched for more than three months and I found it challenging to even take a breath.

"Nice flying, jarhead" Beth said, removing her own helmet with difficulty and oozing back into her seat. She'd been in space for almost a year - the gravity must really be kicking her fanny pretty hard. I snatched the oxygen mask next to her seat and pressed it close to her mouth, and with genuine effort she raised her arms and pressed it closer, breathing deeply like an asthmatic desperate for an inhaler. Her warm eyes whispered thanks and I began the arduous task of clambering out of the space suit - no easy feat in the cramped space with unfamiliar gravity crushing my every movement. Beth had to be absolutely miserable, and I knew she'd never get out of the suit unassisted.

I had no idea if the air outside was tainted with radioactive fallout, but we only had a few hours of oxygen left, anyways. I reached my mind out, looking for the faint tickle of Lothar's presence, but all I perceived was the cooling capsule and Beth's labored breathing. I donned another oxygen mask, mumbled 'here goes nothing' then punched the button that would blow the outer hatch. A loud bang shook the capsule, and a whiff of thermite and tangy citrus drifted in through the open hatch on a gently drifting, thin sheen of purple dust - followed moments later by nervous laughter and the sound of shuffling right outside the craft.

With genuine effort I clambered over to the hatch and peered outside, greeted by a smiling, very ancient, Native American man covered head to toe in the fine, purple powder that defined the entire landscape. If the artist formerly known as Prince had hired a landscape contractor, this would undoubtedly have been the result.

"Howdy" the old man said. "Welcome home."

"Howdy" I replied, "And just where might home be, sir?"

"Last I checked we still called it Earth, young man." He grinned broadly, revealing perfect white teeth that stood out against the dust clinging to his kind, deeply lined face. "But we call this particular stretch of land Sedona, Arizona, if you want to get all technical."

He pulled a blue bandana from his jeans pocket and wiped most of the purple powder from his face. "Lothar told me I'd have guests today, but I really wasn't expecting this!" He cackled amiably, wandered closer to the shuttle and extended his hand up to me. "Jimmy Blue Smoke's the name - folks just call me 'Smokey', though, and you're welcome to do the same. What say we get you out of that Russian sardine can?"

I shook the firm grip and slipped the oxygen mask from my face. "Zack Dalton, sir - glad to know ya. And I guess any friend of Lothar's is a friend of mine, too. I think I can clamber out, sir - but my partner's gonna need some help, I fear."

"No problem - I brought a few younger hands with stronger backs along with me, Zack."

Two young, powerful-looking natives leading horses approached from the right and gave me a friendly wave and smile. "My grandsons - Mark and Chase, they'll help haul your partner out, son. Get to it, boys." The young men scaled the side of the capsule with ease and crouched near the hatch, as if they'd been retrieving astronauts their whole life. I went back inside and helped ease Beth out of the seat. She was sweating profusely and breathing very hard. "If I'd known we were gonna have company I'd have put on something a little nicer," she wheezed.

I guided her to the hatch and the young men lifted her free with ease, gently lowering her to the ground, then pulling me free and doing the same. The earth felt solid and welcome beneath my feet, and I leaned back against the still warm capsule and lowered myself into a seated position. I rubbed my fingers through the fine, purple powder and risked a sniff. It was like putting my nose into a freshly opened jar of Tang; citrusy, sweet and a wee bit acrid, but not unpleasant. The powder was like fluid talcum - similar to the drilling mud oil-field workers used. Slippery stuff, like greased goose liver - and it was everywhere.

I looked up at the sky-skin for the first time from this side, and it was nothing like the view from space had been. I had no idea what time of day it was, but the diffused light streaking across its surface made me think it had to be sometime in the afternoon. It was a dim pall, like a perpetual twilight, but the underbelly of the sky-skin seemed to emit a uniform glow of white light, broken in places by faint, hair-thin cracks of purple that spider-webbed across the entire horizon. It reminded me of a glazed pot my wife had bought in New Mexico years ago; velvety blue criss-crossed with horse hair by the potter that left distinct marks after it burnt off in the kiln. I scoured the horizon but saw no trace of the eye.

Smokey came and sat down beside me as his grandsons helped Beth out of her spacesuit. He offered me a wineskin and I gulped down the cool water greedily, thanking him kindly. It was refreshing to drink something without having to suck through a straw. Beth looked like a rag-doll in the hands of the two strong men, and sweat and purple dust painted her tired face. She looked like she was about to pass out any minute. One of the boys brought one of the horses closer, a big chestnut mare, and I saw that she was dragging a makeshift travois behind her. They laid Beth down on a pile of blankets and furs, and she was asleep before they could ask if she was comfortable. The new gravity was pushing me towards the same state in a hurry. I remember mumbling something to Smokey about the provisions in the shuttle then feeling strong arms lift me - and then nothing but sweet, sweet, blackness.

Chapter Ten
Purple Desert

I awoke to the smell of meat cooking over an open mesquite fire and heard soft conversation off to my right as I rubbed the sleep from my eyes. I was lying on a bed of blankets and furs, tucked away in a small alcove of what was undoubtedly an enormous cave. The fire off to my right cast long shadows high above my head that danced across ancient, deeply red stone. Gravity still reminded me of its presence, and with some effort I took a deep, cleansing breath, gingerly rising on uncertain feet. I stretched hard and welcomed the feel of weight again, then made my way towards the voices I'd heard.

Jimmy Blue Smoke -Smokey- was sitting in a lawn chair beside the small fire with his grandsons, Mark and Chase. Large chunks of meat were skewered on sticks propped up against the red stones ringing the fire, causing my stomach to grumble. Mark grabbed another lawn chair from the cave wall and set it next to Smokey for me.

"Dinner will be ready in about 30 minutes," Smokey said in greeting. "There's a shower at the cave entrance if you'd like to get cleaned up. All the provisions from the Soyuz are stacked there. Beth's going through it all now."

"Smokey," I breathed in reply - "I've been dreaming of a hot shower for almost four months. I really don't think you could've said anything sweeter to me, sir." He laughed amiably as I headed toward the mouth of the cave.

Beth was sitting on one of the many storage containers, wearing only a white cotton towel wrapped around her midsection. Her hair was still wet and water glistened from her shoulders. She looked tired, but content, and smiled as I ambled my way towards her.

"Ain't gravity a bitch," I said, smiling.

"That it is, Zack. Towels are in that cupboard and there's soap and shampoo in the shower stall. You are so gonna dig this shower."

I walked around the corner and peeled out of my sweat-stained flight suit, grabbed a wash cloth and towel from the cupboard then entered the shower. It was finished in rough concrete, closely dyed to match the red stone, sort of like a campground shower but with a rather impressive shower-head more suited to a high-end hotel resort. That first kiss of hot water was almost better than any sex I'd ever had, and my moans proved it. I heard Beth laughing above the deluge, but didn't care. This was awesome.

I stayed in the shower for about 15 minutes. As I toweled off, I idly wondered where the hot water came from. Beth laid out a new set of clothes for me from the provisions, and I clumsily re-dressed, still unaccustomed to my ever-present weight and gravity's concrete resolve. When I emptied the pockets of my flight suit I was grateful to find that package of peanut M&M's Jim had given me. Little orbs of delight had made it to space and back, probably a first for the record books. I tucked them back into my pocket - still not quite the rainy day worthy of their consumption.

I joined the others around the campfire and Smokey handed me a plate with a large haunch of elk accompanied by a large ear of a very-red corn along with a baked potato as lavender as - well, lavender. I'd eaten purple potatoes before - my wife had been a bit of a foodie, but they were never this large - nor remotely near the flavor of this steaming spud of starchy, almost-sweet succulence.

The utensils were equally unique, and Smokey caught me staring long and hard at my knife and fork. The knife was shaped like an ordinary, oversized, steak knife with a highly polished, mesquite heft, but the blade had iridescence to it unlike anything I'd ever seen. Light as a feather and sharp as a laser. The fork was equally light, and appeared to have been sand-cast and polished to an exquisite finish. Bits of red, yellow and the ever-present purple shimmered from the utensils in the firelight as I twirled the fork and knife in the flickering light.

"Hiro Masamune made the blade and my grandson Mark cast the forks," piped Smokey. "Liland is some pretty remarkable stuff, to say the least - you'll meet Hiro shortly. He's undoubtedly still off foraging."

"Liland?" Beth asked.

"It's what we've started calling the remnants of your so-called sky-skin - the purple - or lilac sand that's everywhere," Smokey replied. "'Lilac' and

47

'sand' - Liland. Absolutely amazing compound that's more versatile than manna, as far as I'm concerned. I'll show you some of the pots I've thrown with it - remarkable soil, healing properties, malleable under fire - even functions as a stand-alone foodstuff - wished I'd had it back in my engineering days, and I wish I had a lab to study it further."

Beth's ears perked up when she heard 'engineering' and her raised eyebrows told Smokey to elaborate a bit.

"I was in research and development for an engineering firm for almost 35 years," Smokey said through a mouthful of purple potato. "My specialty was commercial-grade ceramics in every application under the sun. Insulators in electronics, revolutionary building materials, innovations in fluid transport and piping - you name it. I retired 15 years ago and started teaching traditional pottery techniques at Northern Arizona University in Flagstaff, using the science of my engineering skills coupled with the Hopi traditions I learned as a kid."

A shadow from the cave entrance announced the arrival of what I assumed was Hiro Masamune. He was short - even shorter than Mouse, but carried himself with a confidence that betrayed his obvious years under the sun. He looked to be about Smokey's age, which I guessed to be mid to late 70's, maybe early 80's; but the twinkle in his eye spoke to a youthful exuberance that instantly drew me in.

"Nice to see our company finally decided to rouse from their slumber," Hiro said in a thick, Texas drawl that defied his Asian appearance. "Hiro Masamune," he said, extending a Liland-covered hand with a grip that could twist a pine knot into submission. "You must be Zack - and I reckon you're Beth. Sure nice to meet y'all - we don't get much welcome company these days."

I smiled warmly and flexed my hand from the death-grip the diminutive Asian laid on me, then twirled the knife in my palm like a pinwheel - a skill I'd learned from one of my uncles in my younger days. "Nice work, Mr. Masamune - you live up to your name, sir. Is that a sword made from this Liland stuff?" I asked, pointing to the blade sheathed at his waist.

Hiro laughed. "You know your history, Major Dalton - I'm impressed." Masamune was a name steeped in ancient, Japanese history - the moniker worn by its most revered sword-maker in the latter 13th century. "And yes, it is." He unsheathed the blade but it didn't 'sing' like a steel blade as he pulled it free, thrumming instead with a deeper, unfamiliar tone that no doubt resonated lethality. The very smoke from the fire seemed to part distinctly as it swam across the muted, lustrous surface. He offered me the sword for inspection hilt-first, a warning caution in his eyes, and I set my now empty plate on the ground beneath my feet, gingerly taking the proffered blade like it was a delicate, newborn infant.

I'd never held anything so exquisite in my life. I'd been a lifelong collector of swords, amassing a group rivaled only by a few, much wealthier counterparts in Russia and Asia - but I'd have sold my entire collection just to possess this one. It had almost no weight to it, other than a confident *presence* of it felt more than sensed. With one finger carefully away from what was undoubtedly a razor-honed edge, the blade balanced effortlessly with no hint of sway. I backed away from the fire a safe distance and began whirling the blade through a series of lunges and exercises, cringing at the unfamiliar gravity but grinning like a cheshire cat at the deftness and craftsmanship as it blazed through the air around me effortlessly.

"I want one," I moaned. "Got a great spaceship I only used once that I'll gladly trade for one of these, sir."

Hiro laughed then deftly tossed a pine log the size of an oversized cinder block my way in a move that defied his stature. I instinctively lashed out at the log with a swift stroke from the sword and watched it sever against the grain, right through a solid knot, then fall gingerly in the fire, as if laid there on purpose. *How freakin' sweet was that!*

I never even felt the blade contact the wood, other than the faintest hint of an almost imagined resistance. The dopey, astonished look on my face set Hiro to cackling as he unbuckled his sword belt and threw it across the fire to me.

"Welcome back to earth, Major" he laughed. "And consider it a deal - I'd love to see what a little titanium melted down with Liland can wield - but I do have one more favor to ask in trade."

The smiling Asian walked over to an old, particle-board cupboard propped against the cave wall and retrieved a large photo album from the upper confines of the weathered, garage-sale piece of furniture. He sat down in a chair Chase had deployed next to Smokey and began rifling through the pages quickly, pausing at a page rather distant in the grand tome of what looked to be trading cards.

"Side-by-side," Hiro announced with triumph, peeling away the cellophane and producing two baseball-card-sized images I instantly recognized. A couple thousand of them were undoubtedly ash now in the foot-locker of my former Florida home.

NASA started producing 'baseball cards' of all its astronauts way back in the Mercury project days, continuing the marketing effort of youthful appeal all through the modern era. I had my own collection of Apollo astronaut cards - all signed - and I saw my proud jarhead grin and Beth's infectious smile beaming back from what seemed a very distant past. Hiro produced a black Sharpie covered in Liland dust, and I proudly scrawled my autograph across the bottom of the image, passing the Sharpie to Beth.

"These were worth about fourteen bucks on eBay," I quipped. "Pretty fair trade, I reckon, sir. Not too sure what the market's like these days."

"Fourteen bones?" Beth chimed in as she scribbled her signature across the bottom of the card. "Mine were going for at least fifty-seven before Halcyon arrived."

We all shared a laugh at my expense and I sheathed my new exquisite trophy as the tumult died down; the distinctive 'shunk' of the blade riding home somehow announcing a bitter reality that quietly clouded over our pleasant gathering.

Those around the campfire finished their meals in comfortable silence, peppered with light banter that skillfully danced around the precarious and uncertain nature of where we now sat. I pulled the blade just a bit from the hilt a few times, finding comfort as I guided it home with a resolute 'click' that sounded a bit ominous above the coziness of the crackling fire.

Somehow I knew the welcome chime of it sliding home would become an all-too-familiar ring as the coming day's progressed.

Chapter Eleven
Forward

The young men eventually left the campfire and headed deeper into the cave, disappearing into a well-concealed entryway in the cave floor I'd somehow overlooked during my brief wandering.

"Where they off to?" I asked Smokey.

"Down into the main quarters, probably want to play a little X-box before I head down," he replied. "I'll give you the fifty-cent tour in the morning. I think you'll be pleasantly surprised, to say the least. The boys will clear out one of the back rooms tomorrow for you and Beth - if you don't mind too terribly sharing a room, that is. It's spacious, but furnished real estate is kind of at a premium these days, I'm afraid."

"Beth's welcome to the space, Smokey - and I sincerely appreciate the hospitality. I'm sure I'll be content up here."

"Whatever floats your boat, Marine. But if you want to stay up here I recommend sleeping with one eye open and keeping the fire well-stoked. Liland has a lot of good effects, but it's also impacted the local wildlife in ways that are a wee bit... peculiar."

Hiro laughed out loud.

"Peculiar? I reckon that's an understatement, Smoke. Wait'll one of them flying, purple-eyed, squirrels comes wriggling in here looking for a snack, Zack - you'll see 'peculiar' in a hell of a different light, son."

"How so?" Beth asked.

Smokey stabbed a stick in the fire, stirring the coals before he replied.

"The Liland has had different effects on different species," he said in a lecturing tone I knew his college students learned to respect.

"Most of the insect species - and I say 'most' rather conservatively, have remained the same. Some of the bees have taken on the common, purple hue, and they've grown exponentially in the last month. Kind of freaks you out the first time you see a softball-sized, purple bumblebee, let me tell you...." He stoked the fire to his liking then settled back comfortably into his lawn chair, as only a man comfortable in his years could.

"The bigger animals that survived the nukes and didn't die off from the radiation have flourished in a way I didn't think possible. I haven't seen this many elk since I was a very young man," he continued. "Domestic beef cattle seemed to take the biggest hit - ranches south of here that had thousands of head only have a few rangy, Angus bulls and skinny cows left. Oddly, dairy cows seem to be flourishing, constantly foraging on the Liland-covered grass and offering up what seems to be a vitamin-heavy, slightly-pink milk that makes the best damn butter I've ever had..."

"...Sure knows how to wake up a biscuit better'n any I ever had before, for sure..." Hiro added.

The light of the campfire started taking on a rather extreme, violet hue, and the flames seemed to dance much, much slower - as if the fire were somehow still raging, but under water.

"I wondered when he'd decide to show up," Hiro gruffed.

Tendrils of flame started coalescing above the fire in the shape of a disembodied, human-like head.

Lothar.

It had to be him.

Even though I'd never set eyes on the alien, our communication on the station had left me with a definite impression of what the entity 'looked' like.

"It pleases me that you are both well," the flames whispered in Lothar's helium-tweaked bass. "Welcome home."

"Thank you, Lothar," Beth said. "I'd kind of thought you'd be here to meet us in person, though."

"It is not possible. We are... held. We are... studying why, but we are held. It is... curious, and of those that are greater than us. We know not why we are held..."

"Why'd you knock my space station out of the sky, Lothar" I

asked, a bit more vehemence in my voice than I'd originally intended.

"It is not of our doing. It is... interesting. It is... curious. We are... studying. We... do not yet understand." The flames whispered in that slow-mo state of surreal, gyrating flame.

Emotion was an inflection lacking from my previous communications with Lothar, but there seemed to be a genuine befuddlement to his tone. Somehow I believed him, even though my sixth sense was screaming otherwise.

"You must come to us and journey to meet the others," the flame commanded. "That has been seen and understood... it is known."

"Where are you?" asked Beth. An uncomfortable silence lingered for almost a minute.

"It is a place known to you as Alaska," the flame responded, and instantly I felt a compulsion and force pointing a light in my mind that dipped far off towards the northwest; faint, but a compulsion nonetheless glowing in my conscious like a closely-held memory; an internal compass showing me a destination marker almost four thousand miles distant across a landscape vastly different from what I'd known before. Piece of cake and a few hours time if I had a G-4 or T-38 at my disposal - but they seemed to be lacking from my cozy Sedona cave.

"Who makes the journey?" asked Smokey.

"You are... old," the flame replied, "but strong... we are studying. Those that have slept for eons are rising once again... we are studying. You must all journey to us... we are studying... it is... not understood yet with completeness... we are studying."

"Keep on reading and studying your little heart out, Lothar," Hiro quipped. "Who's woke up that's slept for so long? And why the hell do we have to journey all the way to Alaska?"

The flames crackled in their slow, subtle way for a long moment and the image of Lothar in flame ebbed and flowed in the rising heat, as if in contemplation or confusion. "We are... studying. Those known to humanity as Nephilim are once again upon the earth... as they once were. They are... only little known to us. They are of those... greater than us. But we know them... know of them. We remember. It is... not a good thing they have awoken. It is... we are studying. It is... it is... Malathus...it is...not of good. You must come... soon..."

The slow, violet flame yielded once more to a quick, flashing

53

dance of mesquite and pine log's succumbing to fire; and Lothar's visage drifted away in soft, wispy tendrils of smoke.

The silence hung over the group for a painful, long pause.

"I'm just curious..." I said, "Is there a special monthly plan I need to sign up for for unlimited campfire messages, or is that part of a stock plan I should just buy into? Don't want to go over my monthly flame minutes...."

Hiro, Beth and Smokey all started laughing appropriately, but quickly fell into a somnolent silence.

"The sons of Gods are once again risen and walking the earth," Hiro said into the flames, his eyes dancing in the firelight, his mind in a faraway place. "I don't reckon that's a good thing."

Apparently Hiro had attended seminary back in the late 50's, and was a treasure trove of information on what Lothar had alluded to. I'd heard vaguely of the Nephilim, the supposed sons of Gods mentioned in the bible, but Hiro filled in the gaps of my limited knowledge as the fire waned down to comfortable, soothing coals.

Hiro and Smokey finally called it a night, heading off into the depths below the grand cavern. Beth and I watched the dying flames with more than a few thousand questions on our minds, largely unspoken, but the grave visage painted across our faces spoke tomes. She ambled off into the deep recesses of the cave and returned with a huge bundle of furs and blankets, piling it up and making a nest of sorts right near my own sleeping area.

"Kiss my ass, marine - but somehow I'm afraid of purple, flying squirrels. You get first watch."

She was tucked beneath the furs before I had time to chuckle in response, and I sat there for the next few hours engrossed in the dying fire's glow, wondering what tomorrow held. I reflexively played with my new blade and slid it home in its sheath, again and again.

Whatever it promised, I knew I'd be looking upon tomorrow with little sleep and even less confidence. But my repeated pulls of the blade sliding home spoke faintly of purpose and finality and seemed to lull Beth away to peaceful slumber.

Fortunately, as I sat guard around the fire I fed through the night, no freakin' purple squirrels or softball-sized bee's showed their faces. I stood vigil until the first, faint hints of morning, then crawled onto my pile of furs, giving Beth a gentle nudge, hoping giants and figures of legend wouldn't join the cast of my ongoing

nightmares, even for what promised to be a very brief respite.
It was a vain hope, at best.

Chapter Twelve
Luna & Beyond

Mouse was pissed. Really pissed. And no amount of his significant genius could quell his frustrations. He'd been doggedly working for three days with little to no sleep, trying to find a way to get past the dampening field that obscured his view of the station and his friend's demise. One minute he'd been chatting away merrily with Zack and Beth, the next all hell broke loose. Christina had replayed for him over and over what their sensors showed of the space station's destruction before the blackout, and it didn't bode well. He had messages on a thousand different frequencies trying to ping Zack or Beth's I-Pad's - but all he got in return was a chilled, hollow static. He had no way of knowing if they'd made it to the escape pod or if their frozen, bloated remains were now littering the surface of the sky-skin.

A woman with fiery, red curls bouncing entered his quarters silently, watching him feverishly pound away at his keyboard while scanning six different monitors. The equations blazing across the screen didn't baffle her, but she was once again reminded of Mouse's genius. She quietly approached and with a whispered 'hello' began kneading his all-too-taut shoulders.

He reflexively flinched, and just as quickly calmed when he heard her gentle, Aussie tongue close to his ear. To say they'd hit it off in the last few weeks was the friggin' understatement of all time, though not without some peculiar twists. At times Christina seemed to be all over Mouse, other times she was simply friendly. He couldn't figure it out.

He closed his eyes and leaned back, momentarily letting the equations and his frustrations melt away beneath her agile fingers.

Now was one of those good moments.

She leaned in close, ringlets of her fiery, red hair and sweet breath tickling his cheeks and putting his mind in a far more gentler place — but only for a moment — his friend's were counting on him, and he only had a week left on Luna Base before they would take two of the Dwarves back to Earth orbit.

He was growing to trust the brilliant and beautiful Australian communications specialist, but he had yet to divulge what Zack and Beth had told him moments before the meteors tore the hell out of the space station.

His years in government service and as a prodigious freak of intellect had made him cautious and leery, and the revelations of the past month made him even more so - but he wanted to tell her all of it so badly that it ached. His limited exposure to intimacy with others in the past made him all the more leery; somehow doubting Christina's motives as some kind of succubus hell-bent on subverting him and his friends, and he seriously doubted his own, fleeting judgment. And Zack said to watch out for Balthus. Supposedly a reptilian. They were real, after all.

Deep inside he knew Christina wouldn't mislead him- somehow- but these new emotions were all too unfamiliar, and he couldn't put credence into some theory he had yet to prove or disprove. And he couldn't risk Beth, Zack and what potentially remained of humanity's hope upon his fledgling grasp of separating love from lust. No matter what level of genius he aspired to.

He melted at her touch, momentarily closing his eyes and reveling in her scent and the comfort of her presence; a fleeting balm which stood only to further fuel his frustration, doubt and angst.

She sensed his turmoil, leaning in close and wrapping her arms completely around him, her ample breasts across his back eliciting a decidedly more relaxed, albeit electric response that brought a small grin of satisfaction to her face.

He couldn't see the odd reflection of her distinctly non-human eyes in the monitor, nor could he tell that the tongue gingerly licking his ears was pronouncedly forked - but in a quick flash of clarity the obvious finally descended upon him in a cold, sobering wave.

****

"Eamyuot onakeep Malathus, Donasha. Aehad Dharkimon..."

"Zack... wake up... Zack, you're jabbering... up and at 'em, jarhead."

Beth was gently rocking my shoulder and I began to blink the sleepiness from my eyes. My vision was cloudy - and of a distinctly purple hue. I kept trying to focus on Beth, and it took several moments for my vision to adjust. She eyed me quizzically, a touch of concern in her eyes - and she was still in varying shades of violet, like I was wearing a literal pair of rose-colored glasses; I actually reached up to check and see if I was.

Hiro was standing at the foot of my pallet just beyond Beth, also looking a wee bit concerned.

"What was I jabbering?" I asked, rubbing my eyes to try and restore a more normal vision.

"Some foreign tongue - sounded similar to Arabic to me," Beth said.

"Close, Beth. Been awhile since I was in seminary," Hiro added, "But if my ears are still working it sounded like Aramaic. I'll have to roll it around the old brain-pan to try and remember all the words, but I did recognize two of them - actually three, to be precise."

Beth and I both looked to the old Asian, who in spite of my rubbing and blinking looked like a diminutive, purple samurai.

"I believe *eamyuout* is death, *Dharkimon* is love, - and *Malathus* was a name Lothar mentioned last night... the others will come to me - eventually." Hiro wandered off, mumbling the phrase to himself and scratching his chin.

"Your eyes, Zack - take a look," Beth said, concern in her voice, and handed me a signal mirror from her pocket.

I hadn't looked at my face since we were on the station. A good week's worth of beard filled out my chin, with just a little more gray than I cared to see, but the whole reflection was cast in a purple pallor. The gash across my neck from the meteor shower was almost completely healed, although the wound had been more than just a little superficial. Weird.

My eyes, normally a rather vivid blue did seem to give off a faint luminescence. "Some kind of reaction to the Liland would be my guess," Beth said, "But why you and none of the rest of us? Any discomfort or nausea from the accelerated healing? Are you having any trouble seeing?" I flinched back as she shone a penlight in my eye, pain searing through my head and I let loose an involuntary yelp.

"...highly sensitive to light..." Beth said, her scientific mind seeming to not care that she just crammed a light saber through my skull.

"I was seeing just fine until you blinded me, chick!" I spat out. "Everybody kind of looks like Barney the dinosaur, but other than that..."

"...Was it Lothar speaking through you just now?" she asked.

"No" I replied instantly, but somewhat rather uncertain as to how I arrived at that conclusion. My expression must have broadcast my confusion, Beth's quizzical expression telling me to elaborate.

"I'm not sure why I know it wasn't Lothar - I just do."

The answer seemed to slightly appease her and she began to roll up her bedroll.

"Let's get moving, violet-eyes - I figure we've got at least three months of hard travel ahead of us, if not more. No sense wasting time here."

I dressed and began rolling up my own bedroll, thoughts of death, love and whatever or whoever the hell Malathus was dancing through my purple-hued, mind's eye.

Chapter Thirteen
Stormy Skies

I ate a quick breakfast with Smokey in the subterranean facility he called home long before Halcyon came on the scene. Tucked behind Thunder Mountain in west Sedona, the shelter had been carved out of the base of a cave during the nuke-crazed days of the 1950's. Smokey said he bought it cheap in early 1970, and had lived there off and on ever since.

Whoever paid to dig the place out of the red rock must have had some seriously deep pockets. The craftsmanship was immaculate--stairs descending into the lower level hewn precisely by careful hands in the ancient stone. A steel door the size of a vintage bank vault led into a spacious hallway illuminated by recessed, florescent lighting, with another steel door twenty yards further down opening up into the main chamber.

The ceiling was at least 15 feet high, momentarily alleviating any claustrophobia - until you realized you were standing beneath a million tons of rock. It was furnished simply, but not exactly what I expected from a Hopi elder. More like Andy Warhol meeting John Wayne in a battle of kitsch versus sensibility, and neither one winning.

Eamyuot onakeep Malathus, Donasha. Aehad Dharkimon. The words returned to my mind in a flash - unbidden. Smokey saw the alarm on my face and cocked an eyebrow above kind and knowing eyes. "Something on your mind, Marine?"

"More like *in* my mind, Smoke... hard to make sense of it - but I don't seem to sense any malice - more like concern. Genuine concern."

"How about your peepers? You seeing through walls with those purple eyes yet?"

I chuckled. "No superpowers yet, Smoke. Just a purple haze that ... *Aamar aiyt b'meatiyt'eh, Donasha.*"

"Afraid I didn't catch that last little bit, Zack - something tells me you didn't either."

Hiro stood at the entrance to the main living area, looking slightly alarmed.

"He said 'rain is coming, Man', which doesn't make a lick of sense. Haven't seen a drop since your sky-skin showed up - whaddya think, Smoke?"

Smokey rubbed his chin thoughtfully for a long moment then stared hard at Zack.

"If rain is coming - then we'd better start saving as much Liland as we can - you know what water does to the stuff, Hiro. I'll get the boys and meet you in front of the cave. The wheelbarrow is still back behind the upper shower - I think we'd better hurry."

Hiro nodded and headed off to the stairway, Smokey pointing me in the same direction.

"Any idea who's talking to me?" I asked.

Smokey shook his head as if uncertain. "I've got a theory, son - let me gnaw on it awhile before I spook you - best get to harvesting as much Liland as we can... the rain will turn it into a slimy mess, but I don't think it's the bad guys you need to worry about."

"Who's the bad guys?" I asked.

"That's the $100,000 question Zack," he mumbled, walking away.

I trotted after Hiro and met him halfway up the stairs.

"So I gather *Donasha* means man - you happen to recall what the rest of my earlier rambling meant?" I asked.

He continued plodding up the stairs on light and silent feet and gave me a pensive look. "*Eamyuot onakeep Malathus, Donasha. Aehad Dharkimon* means 'Death follows Malathus, Man. Remember Love'."

We continued up the stairs in silence while I contemplated this revelation. Just who or what was Malathus? Did it have anything to do with the Nephilim Lothar had mentioned last night? And just who the hell was using my mind like some ventriloquist's dummy? If they could get me to blurt out Aramaic

61

weather forecasts, what else were they capable of? I made a mental note to be sure and keep Hiro's sword tucked safely away - or maybe keep it close at hand. Not too sure which would be wiser, but I knew I didn't want to become some mind-controlled, sword-wielding automaton.

We entered the main cavern and I felt a familiar sense of alarm - it was the same connection I'd felt with Beth on the station, and knew that something was troubling her. I went to the mouth of the cave and found her staring off to the western horizon. The faint morning light was overshadowed by a wall of deep purple - almost black- that spanned the western sky as far as you could see. Energy flickered through the roiling mass like camera flashes from the crowd in a darkened stadium; long, purple tendrils streamed below the behemoth dousing the landscape beneath it, kicking up a wall of Liland that seemed to feed the approaching storm. We had maybe an hour or two before it hit us.

"Smokey says we need to start gathering as much Liland as we can, Beth. Said the rain will turn it into a worthless, purple sludge. Come on."

I grasped her hand to pull her along and she clinched it, holding me in place. I looked into her concerned, caring eyes. Her connection to me spoke more, and I knew it wasn't the storm she was afraid of - it was me.

"Look at the storm, Zack, and tell me exactly what you see."

"I see a big-ass purple storm a hundred miles wide that's getting ready to piss all over our foodstuffs, Beth. What am I supposed to be seeing?"

"That's not what I meant, Zack. Just describe to me what you are seeing."

I hesitated and stared hard at the approaching storm - looking a bit more intently, but I couldn't pick out anything out of the ordinary - except the constant flashes of energy, and I described it all to her.

The fear in her eyes didn't subside.

"Zack, I don't see any kind of lightning or energy in those clouds."

She let the words hang there for a moment and didn't let go of my hand, giving it a gentle, reassuring squeeze. Maybe more for her than for me, but I still felt a pang of dread.

"There!" I pointed off to a particular bright flash in the sky -

"You had to see that one, right?" Beth just shook her head silently in the negative, looking at me like I was a sad, lost puppy that she couldn't bring home.

What the hell has this Liland done to me?! Who the fuck was messing around in my head?

Hiro approached us with the wheelbarrow, a couple of shovels and a stack of burlap sacks. "Time to earn your keep, boys and girls," he said, glancing towards the approaching storm. "Looks like we're gonna get us one helluva gully-washer." He handed Beth the stack of sacks and tossed me one of the long-handled shovels. "Guess you're making sense after all, Zack. I just hope you're little Aramaic ramblings don't get too complex - I fell asleep in that class a lot. Professor Watkins was an absolute bore..." He wandered over to the nearest pile of Liland with the wheelbarrow, then motioned for Beth and I to get to it. He tossed me a casual salute worthy of Gomer Pyle, grinned and headed back into the cave.

Beth reached up and touched my cheek, and although I still saw fear in her eyes, care seemed to outweigh it - for a brief moment.

I looked away towards the storm and felt an uncanny and ridiculous pull towards it. Probably better not to mention that, I thought. She still thinks I'm somewhat sane - even if I'm beginning to seriously doubt it.

Chapter Fourteen
An Uneasy Calm

Smokey's lithe grandsons made short work of filling all the available sacks with Liland, then began piling load after load of exposed, uncovered piles within nooks in the cave. Sweat matted my hair and shone on my face in a gritty, violet paste. The manual labor felt good, but the mental struggle in my mind threatened to overwhelm me. The storm called to me — literally; it was actually speaking my name with every distant flash and rumble. And it only intensified as the storm drew closer. I focused my attention back on the growing wall of sandbags, trying to ignore the voices on the wind and caught Beth eyeing me in my peripheral vision. She knew I was agitated - that damn new-age, freaking 'link' of ours, no doubt - and I could almost taste her own concern.

I looked at her intently, her face beautiful even though she looked like she'd been partially licked by a giant then dipped in an oversized box of powdered, grape Kool-aid. I reached for her hand and she took it anxiously, her eyes never leaving mine. I relaxed, and tried to open my mind up like she'd taught me on the station. I had to let her know I wasn't going crazy - *or am I?* She sucked in a surprised gasp as the voices echoed into her own mind, and clarity mixed with fear descended on her face.

"You trust me?" I said, clenching her hand tighter and reaching for her other one. Her hand found mine - less anxious than the first grip, and with a decidedly more intimate grasp. Unfamiliar and awkward. But somehow comfortable... and somehow right. And way wrong. She pulled both of my hands to her lips and kissed them softly, her normally stoic, academic face vanishing; a rainbow of violet tears beginning to crease her cheeks, an unspoken and unwilling 'yes' showing in her eyes, and I doubted my own decision for what seemed too long a time.

I brought her own hands to my lips and kissed them chastely, then headed for the cave entrance without looking back, the voices and pull of the storm too overwhelming to ignore. I stopped by my pile of gear, donned a poncho, grabbed a flashlight, a couple of MRE's, canteens and threw them into an old day-pack - my own name repeatedly echoing in a cacophony inside my brain "ZACK! ZACK! ZACK!", accompanied by whispers of *Donasha* cushioning the force. I picked up Hiro's sword - and almost put it back down. "ZACK! ZACK! *Donasha*. ZACK!" *If I'm going to wander out into a freak storm that speaks to me - I might as well have a sword and go out like some kind of comic book superhero. 'Liland Man', maybe? Not quite as cool as Wolverine - but I guess you gotta work with what you've got... what the hell am I saying? I'm about to wander into the desert BECAUSE VOICES INSIDE MY HEAD ARE TELLING ME TO!!!*

I belted on the sword and shouldered the light pack - not daring a glance back to Beth, but nevertheless feeling unseen eyes upon me - and a guilty twinge and flutter in my chest I *shouldn't* be feeling - not for Beth... not now. Too soon, in spite of all we'd been through. *No love for you, jarhead - not until the voices go away - chances are you're about to become Liland-rubbed barbecue in a few minutes anyway - get to it, Marine.*

I sighed and shouldered my way out into the approaching storm hoping I looked more confident than I felt, but also kind of relieved that I didn't have to stick around and look her in the eyes.

****

Mouse took several calming breaths, trying to quell his racing heartbeat and appear as nonchalant as possible. The horrific conclusion that had just dawned on him made his skin crawl from head to toe. *How could I be so freakin' clueless?! Chicks like her do not dig guys like me. What the hell am I going to do now?*

'Christina' still placed gentle kisses and breathed softly on his neck. His mind told him that his arm was shaking like a leaf in a hurricane as he slowly lifted it to embrace her neck, but only the faintest tremor betrayed his anxiety as he gently slid his fingers through her thick curls and laced his fingers across the base of her skull. She had to feel his pulse racing feverishly. She moaned ever so slightly, and Mouse let out a ragged breath. *Now or never...*

He leaned back as slowly as he dared into her embrace, afraid to open his lips and unwittingly free a thinly-veiled squeal of fear, bringing his other hand up to caress her face - stretching back until his hands finally met behind her warm neck... then jerked her head down as hard as he possibly could into the sharp edge of the steel desk in front of him, the bridge of her nose meeting the unmoving steel edge with a gratifying, wet CRACK!!, along with a spray of bright blood that showered him and the monitors in front of him in crimson mist. He rolled his right shoulder beneath her weight and in a fluid up and down motion driven by revulsion, fear and adrenaline began to quickly jackhammer her misshapen face repeatedly into the desk's surface, again and again and again, until the surface of the desk ran entirely red, and heavy rivulets of blood streaked the monitors.

He let the body slide to the floor, the misshapen face thankfully away from him, and he sucked breath in too rapidly as his heart raced out of control. He closed his eyes tight, feeling the warm blood dripping down his face and tried to calm his breathing. He finally forced his eyes open and dared to look down at her, a black, expanding pool snaking through those fiery curls he loved so much - now a matted, ugly thing. He rolled his seat away from the gore, but kept his eyes riveted on what he prayed was the reptilian creature Zack and Beth had warned him about - if not, he would soon find himself locked up in Luna's brig - or worse.

For what seemed an eternity Mouse stared at the corpse and saw no changes, just a dead woman that had been arousing him rather well moments ago - and he feared that he might have just inadvertently murdered the first person to show a romantic interest in him - ever. But a transformation *did* start to happen - slowly, and the guilt on his conscience began to fade away.

He slid back towards the desk - not caring that he rolled through the blood pool, then switched on the comm link to Luna's Operations Center. "This is Mouse - I need Director Salek and Dr. Franks in my room immediately." He released the intercom switch, stood on surprisingly sturdy feet and wandered into the small lavatory - where he began throwing up repeatedly until Director Salek arrived to his quarters - alone.

Chapter Fifteen
Storm Whispers

The chorus of voices stopped ringing through my brain the moment I crested the western saddle of Thunder Mountain. Relief and anxiety hit me with a not-so-soft blow.

It sees me.

I took a swig from my canteen and sucked in a few deep breaths, taking in the sprawling plain and the monster storm obliterating the sky. The energy pulses continued to flicker through the massive cloud bank, but seemed to slowly form a pattern - like casino strobe lights pointing me toward its deceptive main entrance -*Where the house always wins, it's easy to get into - but never easy to leave.*

The red rock saddle dropped to the west at a steep but manageable angle, opening up to a rolling plain covered in yucca, sage, juniper and cacti that slowly crept off westward toward another cluster of smaller, dark mountains whose peaks were shrouded in black clouds. The storm lights seemed to point to the base of the distant hills, maybe ten or twelve miles away, the darkened sky making it difficult to really gauge the distance effectively, but the strobing finger of light leaving little doubt as to where I should go.

I began to make my way down the mountainside, the buffeting wind helping keep me upright in the steeper sections, and the first drops of rain began pelting my face as I made my way on to the scrubby plain. I crossed through a section of barbed wire fence when movement from a cluster of juniper and sage to my right made me jump, momentarily losing my balance on uncertain ground that was no longer easy footing, but becoming slick as a wet ice-skating rink.

Àlo, Smokey's splashed-white, Overo Paint horse emerged from the thicket led by Chase, Smokey's grandson. Àlo nickered a greeting, as if to say "Where the hell have you been?" Chase handed me the reins with a smile. "Grandpa said why walk when you can ride, Major." He climbed bare-footed back up the way I'd come and quickly disappeared in the deluge of rain before I could even say thanks. Thank God for little favors.

Àlo seemed to have no trouble negotiating the snot-slicked surface, while I could barely keep my feet beneath me. Hiro shoed all the horses with his Liland-forged metal, and apparently it was doing the trick. I wrapped my arms around the big horse's neck, grateful for the warm stability. He nuzzled a return greeting then fixed me with an urgent stare - and I noticed his blue eyes had taken on a familiar, violet hue. "You too, big guy?" I cooed, patting his neck then awkwardly tried to get my slippery boots to find purchase in the stirrups - eventually balancing on one foot and using my scabbard to scrape away enough purple slime to get a decent grip. I heaved up into the saddle, scraped my other boot clean, and Àlo immediately set off for the distant hills at a brisk trot, "Glad you know where we're going, Hoss - care to clue me in on what we might find when we get there?" I shouted into the wind, and grinned in spite of my discomfort.

Àlo nickered a "shut up and hang on," then took off across the desert like his tail was on fire. It had been several years since I rode a horse before the few days in Sedona, but after a few rough and tumble bounces I fell into familiar rhythm with his gait.

The rain began to come down in sheets, and I blinked away the downpour - praying with firm conviction that Àlo could see better than I. A bank of Liland dust rose a few feet from the ground, kicked up by the deluge. The violet fog seemed to fight vainly against the onslaught, beaten lower and lower to the ground until it disappeared altogether, fading in a watery blur as Àlo and I sped across the desert.

My fears seemed to dissipate with the dust, leaning in close to Àlo's neck, thrill replacing trepidation - but nowhere near anything resembling certainty. For now I'd simply share the stallion's confidence - it seemed to be the closest thing of substance I could cling to.

The landscape rippled with water and congealing Liland - cacti and skeletal juniper trees bending beneath the wind. The lights in the storm continued to point us west; Àlo never wavering from his break-neck pace or course. The sure-footed Paint leapt across small streams that speckled the plain, bits of driftwood and desert detritus swathed in slick Liland, seeking paths of least resistance. Fat raindrops pelted my face in an ongoing barrage - a cold reality telling me I definitely was no longer on the shuttle lost in some bizarre dream. *Is this really happening? I'm a Marine astronaut - not Don Quixote on some kind of delusional acid trip... why me for crying out loud?*

Àlo began slowing the pace as we neared the cluster of limestone hills, leaving the desert and clipping along a stretch of asphalt washed clean in the deluge, the stark black of the road a welcome rarity in the perpetual violet landscape. His hooves rang like crystal tuning forks across the road, a staccato complement to the shrill howl of the wind and soprano dance of the rain. The lights of the storm thrummed over our heads accompanied by a rolling timpani of undulating, gentle thunder. I pulled on the reins - my first effort at attempting to control the driven course of Àlo - and he acquiesced gingerly - seeming to sense the same presence I did, quickly slowing to a ginger trot, slowly dancing in place to cool himself from the spirited flight across the plain.

Àlo's breath heaved in giant swallows, my knees flexing along with his straining flanks, feeling the strong pulse of his blood flowing in a steady thrum that still bolstered my shaky confidence. The storm continued to rage around us in symphonic cacophony, but a distinct sound like stone against stone - peppered with otherworldly howls that chilled me to the core and caused the sheets of rain to pulse - interrupted the familiar.

D'Leh Bekharboa, Donasha! D'Leh Bekharboa!!

Where the hell was Hiro when I needed him? Another savage peal echoed from a patch of scrub maybe twenty yards distant, and I drew Hiro's sword, a crystalline ring announcing its presence, and Àlo tensed - a waiting coil ready to spring - and he advanced as if in response to an unbidden command as the ringing of the sword still sang on the wind,.

Àlo shot ahead to where the asphalt ended and leapt gracefully - but totally caught me unawares - and I felt myself rising up and out of the saddle, one hand clutching Hiro's sword, the other clinging to the reins for dear life. I felt my feet leave the stirrups, no matter how much I willed them to stay - and I knew this was going to be ugly.

Àlo cleared a tall stand of juniper bushes with the grace of a ballerina, while I felt myself unseated and falling off to his right side like a blacked-out drunk off a barstool, the ground swiftly approaching. I released the reins from my left hand and tucked my right shoulder - *this is gonna hurt like a bitch* - then quickly slammed into the back of something unground-like - and massive; the Liland blade in my right hand skewering whatever breathing wall I'd just hit straight through the back; the blade wrenched from my grasp as I rolled ungracefully to the ground. My eyes registered the big chunk of red rock my head was aiming at a millisecond too late - then darkness.

Chapter Sixteen

Junction

Beth hadn't heard the last three offers from Smokey for more tea. She was engrossed in the flames of the fire and the deluge of the storm dancing across the cave's entrance. Zack had only been gone a couple of hours - and she was antsy and anxious.

Lost in her own thoughts.

Lost in wondering, worrying, planning and trying to process this new reality. Lost about Zack - and *way* lost in what to think about the way he'd looked at her before heading out into the storm. She gazed down at the chipped porcelain mug and the rapidly cooling dregs of the Earl Grey Smokey brewed for her. She held the mug out to him as if in afterthought, and then continued to stare at the flames and the million questions that raced through her mind.

Why am I tied to Zack? What am I supposed to do? Where the hell is Lothar? What will Zack find in the storm? I heard the voices, too - it wasn't Lothar, though ... not to be trusted - can't be trusted, no- Lothar's always been there... trust Lothar... but those other voices were equally compelling ...

Smokey passed her back the steaming mug of tea, and she caught his eyes for a moment in unspoken thanks. His gaze held her -, and the wisdom in his eyes told her to loosen her tongue and share the load - but she still hesitated, blowing over the oily tea, breathing deeply on the soothing bergamot, and let her eyes once again dance to the flames, her analytical mind once again sifting through the myriad questions. Smokey sat back down in his heavily padded campfire chair, a true campfire Cadillac - replete with side desk, lumbar support and three cup-holders.

Fifty years between two wives had taught him when to just shut up and watch the fire. She'd talk when she was ready.

The fire pointed flaming fingers of twisting logic at Beth, each tendril another strand of possibility; Lothar was guiding, he knew the path they needed to take. But she was still an officer in the U.S. Air Force - *if there still is an air force - or a United States for that matter.*

Lothar knew where they needed to go and what to do next, and Alaska would definitely provide more answers. They'd just have to stop at NORAD in Colorado first... *maybe? Why am I balking at that idea? Because you know some windbag General will park your ass in Cheyenne Mountain and you'll get no more answers - THAT'S why.* She wanted to talk to Zack and make sure they were on the same game plan - jarheads could be such stubborn idiots at times... *if he comes back... STOP THAT! - He will be back! Geez, what are you - 14? Get a grip on the emotion, girl!*

Beth hardly noticed Smokey warming up the tea in her hands. After a moment and a mumbled thanks she looked at him and smiled - genuinely this time, and breathed a deep sigh. "I'm sorry, Smokey - just a little distracted."

He patted her affectionately on the leg and sank back into his plush, campfire throne.

"There's more smoke rolling behind your eyes than this fire is spitting out, girl. Don't bear the weight of the world on your shoulders, astronaut genius or not."

Beth seemed calmed by the slight admonition. Patronly advice wasn't always welcome - but it was often sound, if you were wise enough to acknowledge it. She nodded contritely, patted his hand affectionately then jumped right into the practical matters of their upcoming journey.

"You told me earlier that finding a salvaged vehicle or airplane wasn't possible. Why, exactly?"

Smokey thumbed a bit of bourbon-soaked tobacco into an old briar pipe, and then produced a battered, brass Zippo lighter from his breast pocket.

"I've been carrying this lighter since 1963 - but the guts are as worthless as teats on a boar now." He flipped the cover open, revealing a bunch of white-tipped wooden matchsticks instead of the standard Zippo innards. He reached behind his chair, grabbing a small container of lighter fluid, and flipped the little dispenser tube up. "Watch this," he said, "this container is full, but don't blink or you'll miss it... Liland and refined petroleum don't seem to agree with one another at all."

He aimed the container towards Beth's chest and gave it a healthy squeeze. The stream shot towards her and she instinctively backed up with a squeal - but before it could splash into her chest the stream simply disappeared. No "whoosh" like shooting it into a direct flame - it just silently vanished moments after leaving the container. Smokey's eyes brightened at her startled expression and he laughed.

"Pretty weird, huh?" he chuckled, "Wrap your astronaut brain around that for a little while, Missy. You know I'm an engineer - and a pretty darn good one - but I don't have a clue as to why oil, gasoline - any refined petroleum product for that matter - simply vanishes when exposed to the air... it's quite intriguing, really - but it's precisely why internal combustion engines are worthless - and why my grand-daughters pine away for a non-petroleum-based fingernail polish."

Beth reached out for the lighter fluid container, but Smokey shook it from side to side. "Empty as can be and dry as a bone, Beth - as soon as that stream dissipated, so did every other ounce inside."

"Wow," Beth managed to squeak out. Her chemistry professors would've had a heyday with this particular puzzle. "So I guess it's horsepower to Alaska then," she sighed. "Liland seems to have some amazing possibilities - but it also seems to have thrown us back to a pre-industrial stage at the same time - bizarre."

They sat in a companionable silence, listening to the storm noises and the crackle of the fire.

"Smokey," she said softly, "what is real anymore?"

He puffed thoughtfully on his pipe, tiny curlicues of smoke dancing through the lines of his weathered face, and he leaned forward, elbows resting on his knees, firelight dancing in his eyes.

"I don't think I've lived long enough to safely answer that question, Beth," a playful twinkle lit up his eyes, and he grinned through his pipestem, "...and I spent too many weekends with Timothy Leary at Berkeley to be the most credible authority you'll ever find on reality. I introduced him to Peyote, believe it or not."

Beth doubted he was, but she laughed deeply anyway, and it felt good.

"You're full of shit, old man," Hiro said loudly, approaching the fire from the back of the cave, wielding a steaming mug of coffee and waving a silver flask. "Pardon my French, Beth - but he knows *I* was the one that got Leary into Peyote. He was too stoned all the time back in those days - they don't call him 'Smokey' because he looks like that fire-fighting bear, ya know." Hiro's eyes twinkled playfully and he splashed a dollop of whiskey from the flask into Smokey's mug - then held it out for Beth. She took the flask but didn't think Earl Grey and whiskey would make a good combination, holding the flask up in tribute and saying "You're both full of shit - Anthony Russo introduced Leary to psilocybin 'shrooms when he came back from Mexico in the late 50's - I don't recall either of your names in his biography." She enjoyed the look of shock on Smokey and Hiro's face, then took a long pull on the whiskey. Hiro recovered quickly then whistled approvingly with a cackle.

"Now that's a gal I could fall in love with, Smoke - ain't afraid of a little whiskey or calling us on *your* bullshit. But for the record, Beth, Russo was an asshole that still owes me fifty bucks - and *I* was the one that went to Mexico with him in '57. The broke bastard didn't have wheels - and barely enough cash to help me with gas when we came back to L.A. with our new-found 'shroom booty. And no matter what he says, *I* gave Leary a taste of those little buttons of consciousness first. History's written by the dudes who ended up with all the cash when the dust settled."

He sat back in his chair, took a sip from the flask with a pensive look on his face that spoke of forgotten youth, then added an extra splash of whiskey to his coffee. "I wonder how the hell Zack is doing in this gully-washer," he mumbled, staring into the flames, "and just what the hell is driving him and his purple eyes?"

Beth sighed, wondering the exact same thing.

Chapter Seventeen
Tunaki

I came to warm and dry - my head surprisingly not throbbing too badly. No knot on the head, no scratches on my arms or hands, hell - even the wound on my neck was completely healed. I must have been out for days or weeks.

I was lying on a rather large mattress of what appeared to be finely woven grasses, softer than polished silk and quite plush, elevated just slightly above the floor. I was in a spacious, domed room of red stone constructed in a perfect half-sphere. Smooth, unadorned walls rose gracefully to about 25 feet, meeting an inverse, glowing pyramid of turquoise hanging directly overhead. The pyramid emitted a gentle hum, just barely audible and suffused the room with a soft, comforting light that began to brighten as I propped up onto my elbows, followed by a faint chime.

To my right was a large arched doorway, and I heard the distinct sound of approaching footsteps. I sat up completely and a young boy of about twelve years entered the room holding a large, wrapped bundle - Hiro's sword visibly sticking out the middle. The boy was wearing leather sandals that laced crisscross up to his knees, and what looked to be a kilt woven of the same grasses as the mattress I was on, dyed a deep forest green that matched his eyes. His hair was a ruddy brown and hung to his shoulders in lazy waves. He looked a little frightened, and his posture spoke of a false confidence and bravado, and maybe even a little awe. His complexion bore a faint olive hue, like those kissed by the Aegean sun.

More footsteps sounded in the hall, and an older gentleman

with Nordic features, dressed similarly to the boy but with breeches and tall boots entered the room. His hair was almost totally grey, and pulled into a long braid that ran down the middle of a broad back. His beard was full but neatly trimmed, snowy white and framed a genuine smile beneath eyes that carried the same violet hue as my own. He clapped the boy on the back soundly with a hand that looked capable of crushing boulders to dust, motioning him forward.

"Welcome, Major Zacharias Dalton - I am Jacob, and this is Enoch - I trust you're feeling better?" He spoke in a clipped, precise English with a voice like timpani - akin to a British noble that spent a few decades in the Mediterranean speaking more Greek than English. But only my mother called me 'Zacharias' - and only if I was in serious trouble.

"Thank you, Jacob - and yes, I actually feel pretty darn good. And please call me Zack." And I did feel good - almost too good. "And no offense, Jacob - but just where exactly is here, how long have I been out — and how do you happen to know who I am?"

Enoch walked forward and placed the bundle at the foot of the massive bed, and I nodded my thanks.

"Unfortunately, your own clothing was beyond repair - and according to my wife Elaina 'unclean beyond belief.' I think you'll find our clothing to be quite comfortable. If you would kindly dress then meet us in the next room - Viceroy Tarak is anxious to formally make your acquaintance - and I'll let him fill you in on just where you are, but as far as knowing your name - I read the name tag on your flight suit. You've only been out of sorts for a few hours, Zack." He paused and pointed a finger at the corner of one of his eyes, smiling as he turned to go, leading the smiling youth out into the corridor, "It appears you and I have our own notes to compare as well, sir." He stopped and looked at me seriously - "Do not be alarmed at what you see and who you meet, Major Dalton - all here are friends." He waited for me to acknowledge, then nodded sagely and left the room.

I opened the bundle of unfamiliar clothing, rummaged through my backpack to check the contents - the kid hadn't stolen my M&M's - then set about getting dressed. The stockings and undergarments fit me like a glove, and the breeches of a tanned leathery material felt custom made. I'd worn kilts in the past — don't ask, the wife was on a Renaissance Faire kick for awhile — and had little trouble in getting it properly donned. The kilt clasp

76

was an ornately carved red-stone circle of eight interlocking hands clasped wrist to wrist, with bands of silver running throughout the stone. The clasp pin was of a pure, flawless turquoise almost luminescent, and complemented the red and silver stone perfectly. Soft boots of a deep maroon slipped on my feet effortlessly, again as if custom made for my feet. The closest thing I'd ever worn similar were a pair of too-expensive Italian leather loafers my wife made me buy years ago in Florence.

I donned the sword-belt then made my way out of the room and down a corridor that veered smoothly off to the left in a slow, gentle arc, feeling a little like I was heading off to a Celtic costume party. Turquoise fixtures similar to the chandelier in my room were spaced intermittently along the wall, brightening the path as I approached, and then dimming to a more subdued level as I walked by. The scientist in me leaned close to look at one of the fixtures, trying to detect a sensor or some kind of power source, but the placement was seamless between the rock and glowing stone. The kid in me hurried back and forth between the lights, just to see if they would change. They did. *Cool.*

I continued down the corridor and could hear the sounds of a large group engaged in conversation and laughter, peppered with bits of muted music from what I guessed were flutes, horns and strings. When I rounded the last bend, I entered an enormous hall - ten times as cavernous as the largest aircraft hangar I'd ever been in, and it appeared to stretch off into the distance as far as I could see. My jaw hit the ground when I laid eyes upon the occupants gathered around a series of massive, highly polished, red-stone tables encircling an enormous fire pit glowing brightly.

Jacob approached from the nearest table smiling broadly, accompanied by what I can only describe as a Bigfoot dressed exactly like me. The figure was at least 8 feet tall and wide as a barn door, and what wasn't covered in the dark green kilt revealed a trimmed, brown fur splotched with traces of blond and red. Its face was clean-shaven, save for a lengthy scruff of blond beard framing a powerful, lower jaw. The eyes were a dark brown and danced with a light of curious humor and obvious intelligence - and perhaps respect?

"Major Zack Dalton, it is my honor to introduce you to my liege, Viceroy Tarak, leader of the Redstone Tunaki, and Prime Warden of the Sons of Amalek."

I didn't know whether to bow, salute or extend my hand, so I opted for a little of each, stammering out a too-loud "thank you, it is an honor to meet you, your... Viceroy...ness." I spoke haltingly and distinctly - as if to someone who didn't completely speak my own language, and the humorous twinkle in Tarak's eyes brightened. With lightning speed, he grasped my extended right hand up to my forearm with fingers that could no doubt span my entire neck with ease. My hand lay flat against his forearm, unable to circle the massive muscle - and to my credit, I didn't flinch. I didn't have time to.

He eyed me intently and placed his other giant hand upon my shoulder, his thumb across my breast and his fingers extending just below my shoulder blade; then slipped lithely to one knee in front of me. The gathered group of humans and Tunaki took in a collective gasp, the music and laughter stopping in a flash; including Jacob who looked as if he'd been sucker-punched, then all reverently fell to one knee, placing both hands on the stone before them. Even though the Viceroy knelt, I was still looking slightly up to him, but closer to eye level than before. *"Tunaki Basereh, Dakhoa Oleas-Esureh, Donasha"*, he said in a rumbling bass that rang through my chest. *The same language as the voice of the storm.* "I offer you *Basereh* - the binding- to the Tunaki, Zack Dalton." His English was crisp, more precise than Jacob's, and it shocked me. "The stone of my soul is yours to share, *Dakhoa* - 'brother'."

I bowed my head uncertain of why I was receiving these accolades, and even if I should - but knew to refuse what seemed to be an enormous honor might go south in a heartbeat; then I said the only phrase in his language that came to my mind, thinking it might be appropriate.

"Aehad Dharkimon, Dakhoa."(Remember love, brother). He eyed me with a grand smile, replied with *"Apeq Dharkimon, Dakhoa - Defend love, brother!"* then tilted his head back and let out a roar unlike anything I'd ever heard before. Chilling, haunting and thrilling - all at the same time. The other Tunaki soon joined in, while those like me, (human I presumed, one could never tell these days), simply kept their heads lowered and their hands reverently upon the stone. *There ain't no freakin' way Mouse and Beth are gonna believe this, but I gotta admit it's pretty damn cool, whatever the hell just happened.*

I learned over the next several hours why I received the honor from the Tunaki leader - and felt compelled to tell them -

repeatedly- that it was in no way due to skill on my part - just pure, dumb luck. Period. Viceroy Tarak seemed to think fate wove my role with them more than I would acknowledge, and I learned quickly that you simply can't argue with a Tunaki. For one, even the smaller females among the group could rip my arms off and beat me to death with them; secondly, they were logical and kind to a fault, and I finally acquiesced, although begrudgingly.

Apparently when I fell off Àlo's back I managed to somehow skewer a really bad guy - like a Satan-level, Über bad guy - but not really a 'guy' as we understand it - as far from a 'guy' as I could imagine, really - even with all the crazy shit I'd encountered the last few months; tail of a scorpion, body of a winged horse, arms that could crush iron like putty - kind of like a Centaur with a really bad attitude, hell-bent on batting for the other team. Just take a creature from your worst nightmare and supersize it, and you'll get the picture.

Whatever fates there may be managed to make me the killer of Morthos - High Commander of the *Kilkenor; the* top dog of some freaky, winged, scorpion-lion hybrid creatures made in antiquity by someone named Abaddon, a name the Tunaki spoke of in hushed whispers, like gypsies discussing the devil. Morthos had been the first of Malathus - the bad guy Lothar mentioned, who served under Abaddon, and another name the Tunaki didn't seem to like speaking out loud. This was the stuff of fairy tales and mythology, even for the Tunaki - and in no way even remotely resembled the reality I thought I knew. Maybe Beth would have a better grasp of what was real.

What I learned over the next few hours proved as disconcerting and enlightening as my link with Lothar had - and I learned a little bit about why my eyes had started to change. The real bitch of that? Apparently, it was only the first of more changes yet to come. Yee freakin' ha.

Chapter Eighteen
Critters In the Shadows

Mouse desperately wanted a Tic-Tac. And maybe a valium. Director Salek entered the room and looked at the body on the floor with a cool and casual indifference, like Mr. Spock on quaaludes.

"Most unfortunate," Salek said, as if he'd just been informed they'd stopped serving breakfast at McDonald's five minutes ago - instead of looking at the dead Reptilian carcass that used to be his Chief communications officer. "Did it try to kill you? Are you injured?"

Mouse stared at him wide-eyed, shocked by the director's demeanor, and forced his gaping mouth shut. "... no - she... it ... was actually just... never mind... I just figured it out and reacted - is the real Christina okay?" He rubbed sweaty palms vigorously across his thighs, took a few deep breaths in an effort to remain calm and looked expectantly at the Director, who raised a curious eyebrow.

"I only knew of one Christina, Dr. Timmons - I'm not too sure what you mean by the *real* Christina."

Mouse explained the inconsistencies in the behavior 'she' had displayed - and felt confident there was more than one Christina on Luna Base - the vivacious Aussie version and the thing bleeding all over the carpet.

"I feel you may be mistaken on that account, Dr. Timmons. One of the only ways to detect Reptilians - or Drakos- is aberrant behavior - you would perhaps equate it to someone with bipolar disorder or schizophrenia. Reptilians grow comfortable in their pseudo-roles, and when the parameters of their mission change unexpectedly - they begin to react irrationally and inconsistently. I presume that the arrival of your party from the space station didn't gel with Christina's original role as an observer here. Curious, though..."

Salek's mind seemed to wander and he leaned in close over the body, then unceremoniously dug two fingers into the base of her neck without even a slight grimace. Mouse's stomach lurched in somersaults at the grisly sounds of Salek twisting around through flesh, muscle and bone and he thought he might have to run to the restroom again. He sucked a deep breath through gritted teeth and watched the Director pull a blood-smeared, pecan-sized object from the base of 'Christina's' skull. Salek casually wiped the blood and gore on the back of her blouse, revealing a ten-sided decahedron as black as deep space. The very light of the room seemed to be sucked into the matte surface of the object, the facets only perceptible due to the bits of blood and tissue still partially clinging to the surface. It reminded Mouse of the dice he used when playing Dungeons & Dragons as a kid - if he'd been gaming with Satan, that is.

Salek walked into the bathroom and Mouse heard the sound of water running, the Director apparently washing his hands and the curious object. He quickly returned and casually tossed it to Mouse. "A tradition from the old days, Dr. Timmons. When one slew what they used to call dragons - they kept its *korakom* - the "heart of darkness," supposedly it will alert you to the presence of other Reptilians, if the tales are true."

Mouse twirled the *korakom* in his fingers, holding it up to the light to get a better view - but even directly under the desk lamp, the darkness of the object seemed to avoid scrutiny, the separate facets almost imperceptible; he knew it was there in his hand, but it was if it really *wasn't* there; like a radar technician trying to pinpoint a stealth fighter plane at supersonic speeds, one second it was there on the scope, the next it wasn't - his eyes just couldn't seem to bring it totally into focus. *Weird. It's as if it were made to not be seen at all, or ignored. Definitely worthy of more study.*

"I think it best if you not discuss these events with the other members of your group, Dr. Timmons."

Mouse broke his study of the *korakom* and eyed the Director curiously.

"Christina may have been in charge of all our communications - but I also monitor every possible type of transmission in or out of Luna Base- including the contact you had with the space station- and I'm quite familiar with Drakos communication techniques. The only way Christina would've altered her original mission here would've been via direct communication from the Brood Queen or King - and I can say with absolute certainty that that hasn't happened - in the traditional sense, at least..." The Director looked at Mouse intently, weighing whether or not he understood the ramifications of what he'd just said.

Clarity hit Mouse and he nodded quickly to the Director. "Unless she spoke directly with another Reptilian - I'm guessing even you can't monitor that kind of communication, correct? Another Reptilian- Drakos- must have come to Luna Base from the space station."

Salek nodded sagely then approached the communications console, rapidly punching in a series of numbers too quick for Mouse to follow, then rose motioning for him to come along. "My team will take care of this mess - grab everything you need -but we need to get you off the base as quickly as possible... events are unfolding much quicker than anticipated - and that isn't a good thing, Dr. Timmons. Not a good thing at all." Mouse threw a bunch of papers, his laptop and a few belongings into a back-pack and had to almost jog to keep up with Salek's long strides as they strode down the corridor, deeper into the station than Mouse had ever been before, and he found himself quickly lost - and wondering just what Salek meant when he said 'off the base'.

Countless turns and secure doors later they finally entered an elevator that descended rapidly for a *very* long time, Mouse's genius brain telling him they had to be approaching the very core of the moon - or perhaps beyond it. The whining hum of the elevator began to change pitch after what Mouse guessed to be 15 minutes or so, and Salek looked at him with a very thoughtful expression.

"Tell me Dr. Timmons, in all your studies of the strange and unknown - did you ever happen to stumble across any references to a species called the Tunaki?" Mouse's blank stare answered the question. "Do you understand the Aramaic language?" Mouse shrugged an apology - he was smart, but even genius had its limits.

"Are you up for a crash course?" Mouse nodded - not really sure what he was agreeing to entirely - and Salek slowly grasped the sides of his skull, calmly assuring him this would only take a moment. A concussion of intense light flooded Mouse's mind, but he could still see the calm, elongated face of Salek smiling serenely at him. A prickly flood of energy coursed through him, riding a wave just on the cusp of vertigo - and it swelled with a perception that flickered into clarity and comprehension in a deluge of epiphany. Mere moments passed by and Mouse began blinking in disbelief. Salek smiled, removed his hands and moved towards the door.

"You are in for a treat, Dr. Timmons. Prepare yourself, sir, but know that you will be among allies."

The elevator came to a silent halt, and when the doors opened, Mouse's jaw almost hit the floor. "Dr. Timmons, I'd like you to meet Strategos Andrex - High Commander of the Tunaki warriors."

"Holy shit...Bigfoot... " Mouse managed to whisper just before he fainted dead away into the furry arms of the giant beast looming before the open elevator doors.

****

Mouse came to his senses being carried by the creature that had freaked him out beyond belief. He felt like a rag doll in the arms of a Titan, stiffened reflexively and almost fainted again. The Tunaki looked down at him with a keen humor in its eyes, and spread a broad face into a grin revealing teeth that would give a tiger pause. Mouse shuddered, and the giant laughed heartily, lowering Mouse to his own feet with a gentleness that belayed its massive stature.

The beast was well over 10 feet tall, and had to weigh as much as a minivan. You could no doubt mount a flat screen TV on its chest - with plenty of room to spare for a painting or two alongside it. His heavily muscled arms looked as stout as oak beams, and his legs would give a Redwood tree a major inferiority complex. Glossy black hair - or fur? - protruded between a matte-ochre armor that appeared to be boiled leather. Gauntlets that Mouse could've worn around his waist wrapped tightly around

83

the Tunaki's forearms, trimmed in beaten silver in a Celtic-like pattern.

The Cuirass across his chest was affixed with a large symbol of beaten silver, a series of eight hands interlocked wrist-to-wrist surrounding a flaming sword of beaten gold. Individual lappets as wide as a playing card hung from the base of the Cuirass, forming a short skirt that reached mid-thigh on the giant. Each lappet was affixed with individual, flat plates of eight different types of colored stone. Red, green, grey and more. Mouse doubted he could lift it if his life depended on it. Leather sandals wrapped feet that made Shaquille O'Neal's shoes look like baby slippers hanging from the rear-view mirror of a Yugo. They were laced to the knee with more leather than a single cow could possibly provide. A whole herd must've died to outfit this one Tunaki behemoth.

Across Andrex's back was a sheathed broadsword twice as tall as Mouse, and the powerful presence he conveyed left Mouse little doubt that he knew how to wield it with ease. A necklace of hundreds of black beads strung with silver wire hung around Andrex's neck, and upon closer scrutiny Mouse realized they were *korakom* - many Reptilians must've tasted the blade Andrex wore. He shuddered at the memory of Christina's bloody corpse, and then dared to look up into the Tunaki's eyes.

Andrex appeared to be studying him intently, but not unkindly, and that warm humor seemed to linger in his gaze. "I've encountered many in my days, Dr. Timmons - and slain most of them. But you are the first to faint dead away before I could even say 'hello'." Andrex's voice rang like smooth gravel in a washing machine, and Mouse could feel the deep bass vibrations reverberating from his toes to his head. He now knew the Tunaki was speaking in a language similar to Aramaic - and he understood every word as if he'd been born speaking the ancient tongue. Raucous laughter rang from behind Andrex, a large group of Tunaki similarly clad - minus the gilding - scattered in a broad semi-circle behind their leader. None of them matched Andrex in size or stature - but still made Mouse feel like a kicker surrounded by defensive linemen. The smile Andrex wore would've given Marines nightmares, but a kindness in his eyes mollified the effect, and Mouse wondered why he'd even fainted in the first place.

"My apologies Strategos Andrex - the whole other species

thing is kind of new to me. I meant no offense, and please call me Mouse, if you please." The words rolled off his tongue in Aramaic spoken like a poet, and he smiled in delight and disbelief. Who needs Rosetta Stone when you've got an alien hybrid that can painlessly cram a language in your skull in 30 seconds or less?

Director Salek stood beside Andrex, even his massive stature appearing diminutive beside the behemoth. His normally stoic features betrayed the slightest hint of a grin, and Mouse felt like the butt end of some human-related joke.

"Mouse?" Andrex guffawed, "Salek tells me you slew a *Drakos* - barehanded, no less. A rare feat amongst you Toppers. Perhaps 'Mighty Mouse' is a better moniker?" Mouse blushed as the laughter increased behind him, but not unkindly. "May I see the *korakom* you retrieved, Mighty Mouse? I promise to return what is rightfully yours in just a moment." Andrex held out a giant hand, and Mouse quickly dug into his jeans pocket for the odd object, and placed it in the giant's palm. It looked like a grain of black rice in the broad, callused hand. He clenched his fist around it and smiled broadly. "It has been too long since I held fresh *korakom*, Mighty Mouse. We have walked a different path for a long, long time." His face broke into a huge grin and excited goose flesh crawled up Mouse's spine. "It feels good, Mighty Mouse. Very good! Death to the Drakos! *Eamyuot D'Leh Drakos!!*" The encircled warriors thumped their chests and roared in blood-curdling approval. Mouse almost felt sorry for the Drakos - if these guys wanted you dead, that just sucked on so many different levels.

Another Tunaki - female, approached from the right wearing a long robe of translucent, emerald silk wrapped securely with belts of beaten gold and silver, encrusted with hundreds of intricately carved gemstones. Her hair was the blonde of California beach sand, and closely cropped atop a statuesque but lithe frame. Mouse thought she looked pretty - if you thought an anime orangutan was pretty, that is. Her eyes were of a deep crimson hue, and she smiled and curtsied to Mouse, then took the *korakom* from Andrex's hand. A band of what looked like platinum encircled her brow, and she placed the *korakom* into a recessed slot located just above the bridge of her rather delicate nose, then went to her knees and closed her eyes, a higher-primate version of the Madonna in supplication.

"She is Angelicas, Mighty Mouse - a Tunaki Sage-Maiden -

and she can tap into the Drakos' *Korakom* and glimpse all the vile creature knew."

"Okay - sure..." he squeaked - very un-Mighty like, questions racing through his mind as Angelicas swayed slightly in front of him, humming a single, high-pitched tone that soothed away Mouse's discomfort. He thought silence was appropriate and took a moment to take in his surroundings.

They stood within a large room that appeared to be masterfully hewn from the moon rock, but unlike any other part of the base Mouse had seen. The deep grey of the stone was almost blue, and pyramid-shaped fixtures of turquoise gave the room a soft glow. There were no computer terminals or communications consoles to be seen, nothing that spoke of man's touch anywhere. A series of intricately carved stone benches lined the walls, several female Tunaki in a sea of vibrant colored silks seated there and eyeing Mouse curiously. The different colors of their hair- or fur - were almost as disparate as the colors of silks they wore. Some wore belts of silver, and others wore the gem-encrusted gold belt similar to Angelicas, but with fewer of the gemstones.

Broad-swords in stony shades of red, grey, black and green hung on the walls, along with equally colored halberds, battle axes, maces and other weapons that screamed 'I will hurt you' in any language. Elaborate tapestries the size of billboards depicting massive structures from antiquity shrouded the remaining walls. Figures of Tunaki - and humans - were depicted side-by-side in some of the images. Mouse recognized some of the structures - the Giza pyramids, some Meso-American constructs resembling Chitzen Itzah - but others were as strange and foreign to him as the Tunaki themselves were, elaborate palaces with ivory spires that climbed to the heavens, and fortresses that looked impregnable. His wandering eyes were interrupted by a small cry from Angelicas, and he focused his attention back on the Tunaki Sage-Maiden.

"The Brood King and Queen moves, Andrex - and the Kilkenor have awoken from their long sleep. Abaddon's black mists will soon dance through the Toppers' lands. The return is upon us, Strategos. Our silence is over, and we were awoke for good cause."

Angelicas stood up and plucked the *korakom* from its spot across her forehead. She pulled a long, delicate chain of finely woven platinum from a pouch within her belt, then affixed the black die into a setting with a squeeze that would've no doubt crushed Mouses skull. She approached him with a smile - perhaps a knowing smile - no doubt she knew of Christina' s amorous action towards him - who knew what her tapping into the korakom revealed - and she draped the necklace around his neck as he blushed slightly. It was no doubt made for a Tunaki, and quickly swayed most inappropriately and suggestively right at crotch level, which spurred another round of friendly but raucous laughter from the male Tunaki troops and females alike. An older warrior with gray frosting his brow and a wicked scar across half his face shouted something about "that's one way to kill a Drakos I haven't tried yet," followed by more laughs. Angelicas smiled with a maternal glint of compassion in her eyes, doubling up the chain several times so it would ride higher on his chest, then patted it affectionately. "May you fill this with many *korakom*, Mighty Mouse - stone keep you and yours." She bowed her head slightly, her crimson eyes averted, and Mouse bowed low in return.

"Salek - the return has come and Drakos are within your midst. What say you?" Andrex boomed.

Director Salek eyed the group with those giant turquoise eyes. "Stone keep you and yours, Strategos Andrex - good journey, and good hunting."

Angelicas leaned over and whispered in the director's ear, too faint for Mouse to hear, and the Director nodded solemnly. "They will be dealt with, Sage-Maiden."

Andrex moved to the center of the room, pulling the massive sword from the sheath on his back. The blade was as clear as glass and rang like a crystal punch bowl as he pulled it from the sheath and held it high above his head. He let out a roar that shook the cavern and pulsed through every cell in Mouse's body, every hair bristling straight as a plucked cello string.

The soldiers surrounding him ran to the walls pulling weapons from their various places in a blur of efficiency, then encircled their leader like an armed mountain of whoop-ass - with teeth bared. As one they lifted their weapons high and joined in the roar. Mouse thought he was gonna shit his pants in excitement.

"The Tunaki return to reclaim what is ours!! Come my brothers and sisters - may stone guide us on our journey as it has in ages past!!" Andrex roared even louder, the shouts and cries of the other Tunaki making Mouse quiver in deeper excitement and trepidation. "Mighty Mouse - will you join us in the return?" he asked, pointing the massive sword directly at Mouses chest.

Mouse stood there silent for a moment, licking his lips nervously and consciously making his hands stay still instead of rubbing them across his legs as he desperately wanted to; truly uncertain of how to respond, with every massive eye in the room fixed directly upon him.

"Sure," he squeaked, "Where we going?" The Tunaki roared in a delightful laughter that made Mouse grin from ear to ear.

"Back to our home, Mighty Mouse - to Earth!"

Mouth breathed a deep sigh and wondered just exactly how they were going to accomplish that. There was no way Zack or Beth was ever going to believe this - if they were still around for him to tell the tale. He grabbed the *korakom* hanging from his neck and tried to join in the Tunaki roar, raising a fist that looked decidedly puny in present company, a war cry that warbled like a sickly hamster in peril emerging from his lips - and garnered deeper laughter in return than he'd heard all day, some of the Tunaki even rolling on the floor in great guffaws. But there were nods of respect, too. And it swelled an unknown pride deep within him.

I am Mighty Mouse - hear me roar!! His grin was as broad as it had ever been, and he felt better than he had in days. He reached deep inside himself, and from the heart of the moon surrounded by talking Bigfoot's dressed like Xena - with clean skivvies to boot - Mighty Mouse roared.

Chapter Nineteen
The Return

I was drowning in a skyscraper sized pile of "holy-shit-this-is-really-real"; totally lost in mind-blowing conversation with Viceroy Tarak, Jacob and several of the other Tunaki and Cytheran leaders over a meal fit for ten kings. They talked, I mainly stared dumbly like a kitchen sponge tasked with soaking up Lake Michigan. We dined on some things familiar and other things I didn't ask too many questions about, beyond politeness. This wasn't a foodie weekend jaunt to Savannah for seafood with my wife; there were headier matters at stake - but I do recall enjoying it.

I learned Jacob led the Cytheran's, the 'look-like-humans-but-aren't' that had lived with the Tunaki for eons. The Cytheran's were the architect dreamers of the structures of antiquity prior to the great flood - and the Tunaki had been the builders with the know-how to put all the dreams into production. They could somehow weave stone like a master Navajo rug maker. I took a sip of *Grank* from a red-stone goblet, a powerful alcoholic concoction the Tunaki and Cytheran's both favored. Reminiscent of the finest, well-aged Scotch, with subtle hints of cinnamon and sassafras - and kicked like a mule wearing cashmere slippers. I may not be a foodie, but I do know a good drink when I meet one.

"Let me see if I've got this straight," I said, chasing a belt of Grank with a long swallow of cool water. "Prior to a global flood, roughly 26,000 years ago, the Tunaki, Cytherans and humans -

Toppers as you call us - lived together on the planet surface and built these grand structures, the primary purpose of which has been lost to both you and I..."

"Not entirely," Tarak interrupted, "We haven't lost everything to time. We still know how to communicate with the planet, and many of the structures we built were designed strictly for that purpose - we think. It's the exact operations of the specific structures within the Seven Clans that have fallen prey to time."

He grabbed a handful of what I guessed to be a Tunaki Chex-mix - looked more like a rough garden mulch, Jacob assured me that it was. He ground the pulpy concoction with jaws resembling a pit bull on steroids, washing it down with a full red-stone mug of Grank, as big as a pony keg, yet somehow still managing to look small in his hands.

"Much like Topper understanding of your so called seven wonders, your scholars have theories of their creation- some quite bizarre - yet their original purpose and intent has been truly lost through the ages. This is also not unlike our loss of contact with the Eighth Clan - five within earth still communicate regularly...two are isolationist sects, one exclusively Tunaki, the other Cytheran - but the Eighth Clan is more the stuff of legend to us, as well..." He brushed a sliver of a wood chip away from his lower lip that could have easily pierced my hand, then continued. "You're wondering how I know of your ways, yet you know nothing of me and my world?" He looked to Jacob with a smile. "It's nice to have old friends in the Cytherans who blend in a little better with the Toppers – it's given us a conduit into the workings of man to satiate the curious amongst us, and keep tabs on our neighbors. Tunaki have wandered to the surface from time to time over the years - somewhat of a rite of passage amongst a few of our more hot-headed Tunaki youth - they 'streak the top-side', to use a phrase from your own tongue - mainly to taunt any Drakos out of hiding, but never have. Vain bravado and machismo is not the exclusive domain of man, Zack Dalton. Just because we are a separate society doesn't mean we are an idyllic one. We have our malcontents, criminals, lunatics and radicals - not on the scale of Toppers, mind you, but nevertheless still a part of modern clan society."

"That answers many questions, Viceroy, and thank you - but I've still got a few thousand more, if you'll allow it. Especially about these Drakos, what you may know of the sky-skin, why

Jacob hears the same Aramaic speaker I do, about the Eight Clans of the Tunaki, *who* are the Tunaki, what do you know about Lothar and the Orions, why Cytherans look just like humans... we could be here for days, and just where exactly *is* here, anyways?"

Tarak laughed politely at my deluge of questions, and Jacob nodded in patient understanding, droplets of Grank dripping from his mustache. "I've lived among your people off and on over the past five centuries, Zack - primarily in the British Isles, North and South America. We age in similar strides with the Tunaki, like our ancestors named in the Old Testament accounts of your Bible. Methuselah was most likely Cytheran, along with many of the so-called sons of Gods. If a Cytheran or Tunaki doesn't reach his 1000th birthday - it's considered a life taken 'too soon' amongst us. And as far as where here is...that requires quite a bit of explanation...and you really don't want to get me started on Lothar and the Orions..."

'...bbbbbbbBBBBWWWWAAAAAAAHHHHHHHHHHMM MMMMMM!!!!!!!'

The entire cavern reverberated with a vibrating wave and sound of the world's largest fog horn clearing its throat for some final, triumphant peal. Everyone looked as alarmed as I felt - the Grank in my stomach burbling anxiously like a cauldron of worry. Tankards were slammed or dropped on stone table tops, red-stone platters and bowls bouncing across the surface amidst brief shrieks of alarm, the buzz of conversation ceasing instantly, mouths agape and outright fear dancing in fire-lit eyes.

"The Trumpet of the Eighth Clan sounds..." Tarak whispered in a wolfish rumble, "Summon the Clans!!" he shouted, rising to his feet, "To the Channel!"

Two Tunaki ran off at the Viceroys command, thumping massive chests and grunting acknowledgement to the order. Tarak eyed me, nodded abruptly then took off with a stride Àlo would have trouble matching at full gallop. Jacob motioned for me to follow along at a more human-capable pace, his face a thinly veiled mask of concern. I matched his stride - *rather spry for a 700-year-old dude*. The Cytheran and Tunaki gathered around the fire pit descended deeper into the immense cavern along a wide, seamless path of smooth red-stone flowing between fluid, sculpted buildings in a thousand hues of red; devoid of rough edges and what I guessed to be living and work spaces. The Tunaki quickly outpaced the Cytheran's as the so-called trumpet sounded again with a chest-numbing tone that overwhelmed the senses.

"What's going on?" I shouted to Jacob, fighting back the nausea the sound wave induced and a bit too loudly as the peal cut off abruptly, my left hand unconsciously wrapping around the hilt of Hiro's — no - *my* sword — I did give him a spaceship for it after all. And I killed a real badass with it, dumb luck or not.

Hundreds of Cytherans and Tunaki emerged from open doorways and smaller paths abutting the main thoroughfare, merging with the throng moving along at a purposeful but cautious pace - curious but wary. In spite of my own presumed novelty no one gave me even a second glance. Jacob remained pensive. Whatever this horn was, it had to be some kind of really big deal.

"It is the Channel, Zack, a transportation hub of sorts - kind of like a Grand Central Station with links to the seven other clans."

"Is the trumpet some kind of early warning then? Have the Drakos somehow gotten through?"

Jacob looked ashen and his thoughts were elsewhere. "Not exactly, Zack - at least I sincerely hope not. The trumpet marks the gateway for the eighth clan - and it has never sounded before. Not once in more than 26,000 years. Legend tells us that Amalek, the Father of all Cytherans, and a thousand Tunaki warriors walked through the portal after the great flood, to return only at a time of great peril. Basically, Zack - that horn sounding means to us what the second coming of Christ would mean to you." I nodded understanding, recognizing the looks on the faces around me for what they were: a fear of the unknown. Welcome to my world, y'all.

The crowd began to narrow and slow as we approached stairs descending into a vast bowl the size of three Texas stadiums scooped from the cavern floor. I gasped in awe and paused at the top of the stairs with Jacob, others streaming by us politely but hurriedly. Seamless stone benches concentrically ringed a vast plaza rapidly filling up with tens of thousands of Tunaki and Cytherans approaching from multiple avenues. Seven massive obelisks, measuring at least a hundred feet at the base, of different types of brightly colored, highly polished stone rose in a crescent moon pattern from the plaza floor, their pointed peaks hundreds of feet above the bowl's lip, clambering almost beyond sight.

Jacob tugged at my sleeve, and I ambled down the broad

stairs, my eyes soaking up the immense red-stone city sprawling off to all points of the compass, the obelisks a neon contrast to an otherwise crimson landscape. Rounded domes, fluid minarets, willowy spires and geometric curiosities in all shades of red reached for the far distant cavern ceiling. How could such a vast place exist and man never know anything about it? My roller coaster ride of revelation didn't look to be stopping anytime soon.

It took us several minutes to descend to the lowest level where the obelisks were arrayed on the elevated grand plaza of the Channel. Viceroy Tarak stood ten paces from the face of the grey-stoned, center obelisk, appearing vibrant in spite of the breakneck pace he'd no doubt managed to get here. A horseshoe-shaped gateway like a train tunnel in the obelisk base opened up to nothingness, a dark void that seemed to sparkle with wisps of ebony blue - similar to the energy I saw in the storm clouds, but Beth couldn't. Above the horseshoe arch was an elaborate curved trumpet in a metallic, matte grey the size of a tour bus, grey dust shimmering in settling clouds around it.

At the corners of the obelisk stood a Cytheran and Tunaki pair, their hands placed in palm-sized niches on the adjoining faces. Their eyes were closed, heads leaned back, the Tunaki towering over the Cytheran standing at his feet. They began chanting a throaty overtone that brought to mind Tibetan throat singing- if King Kong were singing bass. As the harmonic overtones merged the hair on my arms and neck began to rise, a tickle spiraling up my spine. The deep blue shimmers within the gateway took on more light and action, an etch-a-sketch portrait of blue and black done all at once. Outlines of hundreds of figures - presumably Tunaki - began to take shape, quickly washed out in an immense flood of white light that momentarily blinded me - super purple vision or not.

As I blinked my eyes back into focus, the biggest Tunaki I'd ever seen - as if I'd seen many - stood before a menacing half-ring of battle-clad warriors. And when I say menacing I mean these guys made Klingons look like Girl Scouts. Wimpy, geeked out Girl Scouts. With asthma. The big one in front strode forward purposefully toward Viceroy Tarak, some kind of dog at his heels... *wait, that's not a dog - that's freakin' Mouse! Mouse!! Holy shit! What the hell is he doing here?!*

Mouse's face lit up with equal astonishment when he saw me, and he ran forward and hugged me tighter than I thought his nerdy little arms were capable of. I embraced him with equal vigor, surprised at how grateful I was for this tiny bit of familiar reality. "You're alive, you're alive, you're alive..." he repeated over and over, "I knew it!" He leaned back, laughing tears with a grin a mile wide, his arms shaking in his delight as he held me at arm's length. Damn good to see a normal, friendly face in this FUBARed world I supposedly thought I knew.

"Who's your friends?" I nodded my head warily toward the Tunaki arrivals, who began to emerge from the gateway in a steady stream behind the crescent moon of what must be a senior cadre of warriors. Brightly clad females interspersed with other soldiers, elder Tunaki in shades of brilliant white fur wrapped in a kaleidoscope of colored silks and gems, all merging out on to the grand plaza; from the rear a number of regally clad -and for lack of a better term - giants - emerged. No-shit giants.

They were larger than the Tunaki on this side of the Channel, resplendent in cloaks and gowns as decadent as any Tudor noble, but their features were human, just on a grandiose scale. The faces of Roman gods depicted by the greatest Dutch Masters - Michelangelo's *David* sprung to brilliant life in vibrant, living flesh.

Mouse's reaction of wide-eyed wonder mirrored my own, he must have not have been traveling with this Twilight Zone caravan long. Mouse looked about ready to reply when we noticed every eye present focused intently on us. Not with any menace or contempt; more like spectators appraising the opening act before the headliner takes the stage. We might not have a star on the dressing room door, but we did manage to somehow make the playbill. God, please don't let us crash and burn on opening night!

The tallest and most regal of the giants in the forefront of the group leaned toward Mouse and I, a ginger smile splayed out on a face sculpted from creamed alabaster. Glacial blue eyes radiated a palpable and breathtaking *kindness* that sucked me into an overwhelming sense of calm and peace — What I'd always hoped in my secret heart-of-hearts what it would be like to meet Jesus — albeit this version of my secret, spiritual yearning happened to be before a clean-shaven, blond, Adonis-like figure of majesty. No simple shepherd's robes or lengthy beard, but nevertheless what simply had to be defined as "God-like".

In a flash I knew without any doubt the beautiful being

smiling warmly at me was the voice I'd been hearing the past few days. "Amalek," I gasped, in unison with Jacob, who had silently walked up beside me, a placid adoration alight on his Cytheran face. Amalek smiled like Santa at a bright-eyed toddler who made it to the top of the good list, then placed a skateboard-sized palm atop Jacob's skull, and then on my own as gently as stroking a newborn kitten.

Warmth and light blocked out all vision and perception. I felt purposely drawn through a sea of serenity, acceptance and absolute bliss. It's so hard to describe this place or plane or whatever it was without feeling completely inadequate to the task — Willingly drowning in a milk chocolate soup of unconditional love is about as close as my feeble mind can seem to muster. No fears, no concerns - no questions, really... just a certainty of... everything, to be honest. In a loving flood of instant revelation I knew the answers to every puzzle I'd ever pondered; about creation, the cosmos, consciousness, women, God, physics - everything filled me to bursting and just kept coming and coming, like trying to drink water from a hundred gushing fire hoses - all at once.

Amalek lifted his hands and the deluge of omniscient knowledge ceased flowing. Whispery tendrils of data floated into the recesses of my mind, beyond the veil of conscious thought - the clarity I'd just sank my teeth into dissipating along with it. Where obvious answers had been, only whispers of possibility lingered. An echo of solutions heard miles away, uncertainty and hesitation replacing what momentarily had been absolute truth. I longed to tap back into this wellspring of knowledge, like a child given the greatest lollipop ever but only allowed a single lick before having it taken away.

"You do remember love, Man," Amalek said, "And you, too, Cytheran. You know what must be done. I must leave this place now, for when I am here, so is Abaddon, but he can only remain as long as I do. Those that are with him are greater than those with us, for the moment - but you will do what must be done." Amalek looked to the massive Tunaki who'd accompanied Mouse and placed a hand upon his shoulder. "Watch over them, Strategos Andrex - the final battle comes, and they are stone-worthy." The Tunaki bowed reverently and Amalek and the other giants with him turned back towards the Channel gateway. He paused, turning to the gathered masses and spoke in a clear voice

95

that rang to every ear in the room. "Learn once more who you are. Remember love, and the burdens you swore to bear." En masse the giants disappeared in a shimmer of blue energy before even gracing the portal. I looked at Jacob and Mouse, internally grasping for the next steps Amalek said I supposedly knew.

"We need to go and get Beth and the others and bring them back here - right now." I wasn't too sure what drove this compulsion, but Jacob nodded in instant agreement and Mouse simply stared at me in awe. "What?" I asked.

"Sorry, Zack - you're just... glowing like the biggest lightning bug I've ever seen." I looked at my hands and arms, and they *were* glowing with a soft, violet light that slowly slipped back into my normal skin tones. "Cool" I whispered with no hint of fear, and eyed Viceroy Tarak. "Can you take me to my people, Viceroy?"

"That is my task, Topper - or did you not hear the guidance of Amalek?" The massive Tunaki Amalek called Strategos Andrex spoke with a voice that could collapse caverns, and bore a steely conviction in his eyes. Viceroy Tarak nodded a meek acquiescence and I attempted a smile at the imposing Tunaki warlord.

"Then let's roll, Strategos Andrex. Seems we have a lot to do - not real certain about all the 'whats', but I know there's a whole lot of them." The confidence in my voice rang a lot louder than I truly felt, and I hoped my uncertainty wouldn't somehow once again rise to the surface.

"You may *roll* if you please, Topper, but Tunaki warriors do not *roll* - we march boldly and run faster than the wind. Come - let us find your friends and hope cursed Abaddon has not yet set his soulless gaze upon them." He spat and looked at several of the Red-Stone Tunaki leaders with disdain plain upon his face. "As Strategos I answer only to the High Councilor - and before me stands a *Viceroy?* I will know of why you failed to maintain the Eight Burdens, *Viceroy* - but for now I will serve this stone-worthy Topper, as Amalek decrees. And you will accompany me."

Tarak nodded to the massive warrior, recoiling at the power and depth of his voice, and I actually felt sorry for him. Then I took a deep breath myself. *I can do this. Whatever this is, I can do it.* I had a little more knowledge than I did this morning, answers to some questions lingering in shadows in the hidden paths of my mind, but once again I was heading boldly down a path of uncertainty, only knowing I had to — no, I *wanted* to — follow it through its course. Not like I had any other plans or anything. I'm guessing the whole naval aviator and astronaut job market was about as dead as the dinosaurs. *Time to dance with Bigfoot and the immortals. I just really hope the universe knew what the hell it was doing when it tapped me on the shoulder. God please help us all.*

Chapter Twenty

Blood and Sage

I left the plaza with a lot more eyes on me than when I'd first arrived. I can honestly say I now know how Elvis and the Beatles must have felt. And Jacob must have felt it too. Every furry-armed Tunaki and bright-eyed Cytheran wanted to meet or talk to the two actually touched by Amalek himself. And there were a LOT of furry arms and bright eyes in that stadium. Andrex became impatient with our progress and surrounded us with an honor guard of twenty Tunaki warriors that plowed us through the curious like Moses through the Red Sea. Mouse and I had to maintain a brisk jog out of fear of getting run over by our own protectors.

As we crested the top of the stadium stairs, a warrior with greying temples and a wicked scar slashing across his face turned to Andrex. "I smell Drakos, Strategos."

Andrex never paused in his stately gait, sniffed the breeze heavily, and then looked to his right. "Seek," he barked in a smooth, even tone, and instantly our cocoon of twenty warriors became ten, the entire right flank peeling off in the direction Andrex looked, but filled instantaneously with warriors from the center and rear, maintaining a bubble of protection around our small cadre.

"*Eamyuot D'Leh Drakos,*" Mouse mumbled, an odd grim light on his face, sucking wind from the brisk pace — when I realized I'd understood him - AND Andrex AND the old warrior with the

98

scar. And they'd all been speaking that odd Aramaic. "Death to the Drakos," I said, grinning broadly and gasping a little myself. Mouse looked at me like I was a little off. "I understood you, Mouse - and the other Tunaki speaking Aramaic - I couldn't do that this morning, before the whole thing back there...."

"...Neither could I," Mouse replied grinning, "We sure as hell ain't in Kansas anymore, Toto."

What other 'gifts' did Amalek give me with that touch? And what was it gonna cost me?

"It will cost you everything and nothing, man." Amalek's voice spoke clearly in my mind as if in response, but I somehow knew that it was merely a reflection of Amalek, and not him directly. Kind of like Siri on my iPhone. Some questions might be answerable from remnants of the 'touch', and I guessed Amalek would only answer certain questions - I felt a burning conviction that choice somehow still played a big role in things to come.

We hurried on through the main thoroughfare, stopping only when we arrived at the tables and fire-pit I'd dined at earlier. Mouse took a seat at one of the tables, breathing hard from the jog, and Jacob and I joined him - Jacob filling us a couple of red-stone mugs from a pitcher of water. Viceroy Tarak and Strategos Andrex were embroiled in a rather one-sided, heated conversation. Tarak looked somewhat defiant but also like he wanted to crawl under one of the nearest tables, and Andrex was a volcano well past a much needed eruption. Bits of his tirade made it to our ears in snarled Tunaki tones, "...How can you possibly not know the Eight Burdens?!... the Kilkenor were here yesterday and you mention this now?!... that Topper slew Morthos? What of the bloodstone? Fetch it now!... These Toppers are more Tunaki than you!! ...Stone-cursed, wasted fur-bags unfit for breathing!!... do the Kenawak still live? Good, at least the blessed Creator did not let you foul it all up - summon the Kenawak masters with 50 mounts for my guard at Tenegress Prime, and suitable mounts for ten little ones," Andrex drilled a finger the size of a baseball bat onto the Viceroy's chest, accentuating each 'YOU' with pokes that would have punctured a semi tire, "...Then YOU will return to Channel Plaza and seek out Elder Denwayn - and YOU will beg him to teach YOU all about who YOU really are. Do YOU understand me, Viceroy Tarak?" I felt the last poke from 15 feet away, and heard Tarak grunt under the assault.

"Stone Clear, Strategos - it shall be done as you say," he wheezed, scurrying off and still looking a whole lot more proud than I would have under that kind of drumming. Dude was gonna have a bruise the size of Montana across his chest, and no doubt his ego was on the receiving end of a marathon gang-bang at a nympho convention that didn't look to let up any time soon. *Party's over, boys and girls - Mom and Dad got home a little early - and I'm thinking they're pretty pissed about how you took care of the house.* Guess I shouldn't judge - it wasn't as if humanity had actually stuck to its supposed original dictates, either. Whatever those may have been. What was the old joke? *"Jesus is coming soon - and boy is he pissed."* The Eight Burdens must be similar to our own Ten Commandments, a list of thou shalts and shalt nots - and there were eight Tunaki clans. Maybe each clan bore one of these burdens?

In two strides Andrex was at our table giving me a VERY hard look. "You and I, Topper Zack - we will not be friends, I think. I cannot be friends with those who would steal from me - and you have stolen a treasure I prize above most." I choked a little on the water I was sipping on - my normally quick-witted tongue tangled in an inexplicable knot. Andrex broke into laughter and slapped me on the back hard enough to rattle my teeth. "I walk in a distant place for eons and the first two Toppers I meet are more ferocious than any Tunaki Warrior. Mighty Mouse slays a Drakos bare-handed, and Zack Dalton singlehandedly slays Morthos, the most hated spawn of Abaddon even in my own time. THAT is what you have stolen from me, Topper Zack. Vengeance." Tunaki humor and camaraderie would definitely take a little getting used to. My ears were still ringing.

Eight of the ten warriors who peeled off after the Drakos scent approached the tables, the scarred and wizened older warrior holding a hand out to Andrex with four of the odd, matte-black die in his sandpaper palm.

"Four fell easily, Strategos - all wearing Cytheran faces. One in Tunaki face has fled deeper into the city, but Curtz and Taka will slay it in short order." Andrex plucked the die from the warrior's palm, and motioned for a female Tunaki to approach. "Well done, Brizzock. We ride Kenawak today, old friend - summon scouts for a troop-level foray from Tenegress Prime - pick your best, Brizzock, there are Kilkenor craving death. But this Topper Zack Dalton..." Andrex nodded his oversized Chewbacca head at me,

"...has made our job much easier. He slew Morthos with a single stroke yesterday." Brizzock arched his one good eyebrow in genuine surprise, the scar running across half his face paling slightly. He nodded to me in an almost reverent bow, then slammed an iron fist across his chest in salute, along with all the other gathered warriors. "Those who steal from us cannot be our friends, Strategos - I hope this Topper knows that." Brizzock's voice was sandpaper over rough gravel, and his grin brought to mind a scary, fuzzy clown. Tunaki humor definitely was an acquired taste.

****

Mouse filled me in on *korakom*, Tunaki sage maidens, and told me about his adventures and misfortunes on Luna Base as we trotted along to Tenegress Prime, which was just a fancy name for the gateway to our place on Earth. Jacob told us each colony had three Tenegress gateway's bridging the Tunaki and Human planes: the Prime, Alpha and Omega access points. The colonies were not just below the surface of the planet, they were *beside* our own plane - sharing the planet with us, but within a dimension just slightly out of sync with our own. That's how they seemingly stayed beyond our awareness all these eons.

I was trying to focus on teaching Mouse how to properly mount a spirited Cytheran thoroughbred, but kept getting distracted by the massive Tunaki warhorses - Kenawak - impressive, all-white beasts standing at least 25 hands; powerful chests, tightly braided manes with long, pearlescent hair flowing around their cannons and fetlocks. They were almost too pretty to be warhorses, in my opinion - a sentiment seemingly shared by Strategos Andrex. Many of the Tunaki were shearing the silken hair from the Kenawak's legs with diamond-bladed daggers I could've used as a short sword, shaking their heads in disbelief at the too-pretty beasts.

"It is a wonder Abaddon does not already rule with such fools left as stewards of Earth... stone-cursed, fluffy show ponies..." Andrex grumbled, more to himself than anyone else, deftly shaving the downy hair from the rear leg of his mount. The Kenawak Master was a frantic Cytheran who couldn't seem to quit waving his hands, and almost passed out when the warriors began shearing the soft hair from the massive beast's legs, screaming they were ruining his greatest investment. One look from Andrex sent him scurrying back to the stables in barely muffled sobs.

Àlo seemed pleased to see me, and wasn't a bit skittish in the presence of the strange Kenawak's that dwarfed him, nor did he shy away from the Tunaki warriors who patted him affectionately, staring curiously at his purple eyes. We all mounted and rode through a veil of shimmering crystal in the cavern wall and the next moment were on the Arizona plain, a sheer wall of black rock at our backs, shaking off the chill of passage just outside the stony landscape of the resort at Enchantment. The experience was like those first seconds walking into a department store on a hot day in Phoenix. One second you're outside sweating balls, the next you're awash in a blast of welcome, frozen air.

I shook off a tingle of chill and pointed distant Thunder Mountain out to Andrex, and the group picked their way eastward through the rocky terrain. When we reached flatter ground, twenty warriors galloped off ahead of us in a wide arc, staying about a quarter mile ahead and abreast, wooly Tunaki heads scanning the horizon, sensitive noses seeking out any Drakos or Kilkenor on the breeze. Andrex rode to the far left on a Kenawak stallion that *didn't* look as pretty as the others; downright ugly as a matter of fact, but it seemed to somewhat placate the grumpy warrior - just a tad. The Tunaki sage-maiden Angelicas rode beside him on a much smaller Kenawak mare, the last beast still replete with flowing fetlocks; her eyes were closed and she swayed as she examined each of the korakom Brizzock had claimed earlier. Jacob, myself and Mouse took up the center, with Brizzock riding close to Mouse's right. A solid line of mounted Tunaki took up the rear - I couldn't imagine a safer place to be in the whole world. When these guys had your back, you could sure breathe a little easier.

Evidence of the previous day's deluge was all but gone. Puddles of gooey Liland filled up hollow spaces here and there, but the rain had washed the vast majority of the vital, purple dust away. I hoped Smokey's stockpiling proved wise.

"Mighty Mouse," rumbled Brizzock like a voice from the heavens, "I hope you do not deem me impolite, for I would never tell anyone who has slain a Drakos barehanded how to fight - but we will soon face Kilkenor - and they do not die as easily by hand alone." The warrior eased his mount a little closer to Mouse, a tractor trailer merging lanes beside a Cooper Mini, and handed down a claymore-like broadsword in a beautifully finished scabbard of patinated silver. Delicate runes of turquoise embellished the locket and chape, and Mouse, jaws wide open, definitely had his Geek-meter fully pegged.

If I didn't already have a cool sword I would've been quite jealous, and I hadn't even seen the blade yet. I bit back my curiosity, instead whistling approval, and Mouse beamed like a proud, new parent. One of the smartest men ever to attend MIT and he was as giddy about sharp, shiny objects as I was. You gotta love a buddy.

"Brizzock, this is simply too much - way more than I can accept..."

Brizzock grunted a harumph, "Just quench its thirst for Drakos and Kilkenor blood, Mighty Mouse. Our debt is to the Creator - not one another," adding solemnly and with a stern one-eyed gaze, "May you live long enough to never love using this, little brother. Stone keep you." He nodded, then guided his mount forward to the right flank line with his fellow warriors.

Mouse thanked him as he rode off, then focused his attention on the blade, flashing me a wolfish grin. "I'd like to see you try and spin me 'til I puke with this in my hands, asshole."

Jacob laughed and I patted the hilt of my own sword, "Oh don't you worry, Minnie Mouse, we'll dance - you can bet on it. Just remember that a keyboard and some fancy code won't get you out of this mess. And I don't plan on hugging and kissing your neck anytime soon to give you such an easy target, pal. No way." Mouse guffawed with a gleam in his eye.

"Bring it on, Zack - you just tell me where I need to stand and defend myself - should you happen to fall off that horse." I laughed along with both of them. It was damn good to have Mouse back. Mighty or not.

Àlo began to nicker and prance, ears twitching nervously, the other horses shying away from the fidgety Paint. "Somethings up," I said, clenching my knees into Àlo's flanks — just in case — no way in hell was I gonna fly out of this saddle, especially after what Mouse just said.

The report of a rifle cracked through the air, followed by a quick volley of staccato small-arms fire - close by. I felt for Beth, and terror and alarm punched into my chest. I wanted to shout a warning - but the Tunaki were already spurring their massive Kenawak's forward, weapons at hand in a silent flash.

Àlo strove to match them as best he could. In my mind I screamed out to Beth "We are almost there - hang on. Don't shoot the fuzzy ones! They're the good guys!!" I put as much force behind the thought as I could muster. I was grunting more like I was constipated rather than trying to convey a sense of extreme urgency and calm.

Rifle fire continued as we crossed the ridge, but no rounds whizzed by our heads. Whoever was on the business end of the rifle must've known what they were doing. I kept repeating the warning in my head over and over when clear as a bell I heard Beth in my mind - *"Enough, okay? I got it - big, fuzzy guys on giant white horses are friendlies - just hurry - we don't have a lot of ammo."* I recoiled at the clarity and brevity of the contact, mumbled a muted "okay," then drew my sword, for the first time wishing it was a .45 or .9 mil instead. Unfortunately, 'Saber mounted cavalry techniques hadn't been a course at the academy for about a hundred years - but thank God for rich buddies that suckered me into playing polo. If I was gonna get killed, at least I'd look like I half-ass knew what I was doing.

Mouse shot off behind Brizzock looking like a seasoned jockey on derby day, his new blade bared — appearing to be handled quite capably, to my surprise and relief.

I focused on the cave entrance, a hundred yards up a scree and boulder-strewn path that switched lazily up the steep slope. Kilkenor blocked the entire path, massive black scorpion tails facing us as they clambered up through the rocks, yet to encounter the first of the quickly approaching and silent Tunaki warriors.

"Eamyuot D'Leh Kilkenor!!" roared Andrex as the first of his warriors plowed through the rear of the unholy beasts. Their trunks were of equal size to the Kenawak, powerful rear legs of a draft horse, front paws of an agile lion, appearing even larger with their massive scorpion tails curled skyward.

Boiled leather armor covered massive chests rivaling Andrex in stature, with muscular arms gripping long, jagged blades of dirty bronze in clawed hands. Dreadlocked manes of black, orange and muddy tans framed hideous faces - 'Eddie' from the Iron Maiden album covers came to mind - albeit with the teeth of a saber toothed tiger and a winged body designed by Dr. Moreau on acid.

With each crack of the rifle I saw a Kilkenor stumble - about once every five seconds - with another clambering over it as if it were simply part of the terrain to overcome. One leapt to the air with a powerful beat of wings that must have spanned twenty feet or more - then crumpled in a heap as the rifle wielders continued to find their targets.

Tunaki blades decimated the Kilkenor line with ease, no hint of a pause as they plowed madly into the now-alerted creatures. The beasts closest to the cave never faltered, trudging upward as those around them continued to fall. Others closer to the Tunaki assault turned soulless eyes and feral grins to the new threat. I completely severed the tail of the Kilkenor Àlo picked out just as it was beginning to turn towards me, my Liland blade sizzling through its blackened telson with fluid ease - Jacob cleanly relieving its head from its shoulders as he followed along closely behind. I urged Àlo along, the rest of the ascent a blur of crackling Kilkenor blood singing from my blade amidst screams, guttural howls and rifle fire.

I don't recall dismounting, but soon found myself standing over a badly bleeding Beth at the cave's entrance - the sticky blue blood of at least half a dozen Kilkenor I'd waded through and killed covering me. In mere moments I was holding her, desperately calling for help and vainly trying to stop the blood pouring out of her with every weakening heartbeat, the red flow painting a grisly channel through the blue kilkenor blood pooling beneath us.

A teardrop bead of sweat trickled down the bridge of my nose, and the world went silent around me save for the rapid thrumming of my pulse. Dust motes of Liland stood suspended in front of my face, and the drop of perspiration that fell from my nose remained motionless just below my mouth, suspended in free-fall as if I were back on the space station. I tried to move my neck, but felt like I was kneeling in a cocoon of partially-set concrete.

I panicked and tried to will my limbs - anything - into motion, but only my eyes and innards seemed unaffected by whatever gripped me, and Beth remained lifelessly still in my arms. The din of battle was gone, figures around me frozen in time and clueless to their predicament. Hiro was in mid-stride rushing towards me to help with Beth, looking like a Samurai version of the Heismann Trophy, but his eyes were fixed and unmoving with no hint of panic or recognition. Movement to my right caught my attention, but no amount of will would free me from the unnatural grip surrounding me.

Purposeful, unhurried and heavy steps sounded across the cave floor, the confident stride of something huge. New panic surged within me as whatever it was moved closer. I tried to shout, scream - anything - but remained completely immobilized.

The long strides drew closer, peppered with an intermittent *SNAP* like a brass weight tumbling on a glass table top between heavy footfalls. *A cane?* I felt the pressure of an immense hand on my back, but was so frozen not even my skin could crawl.

Internally I was struggling against the invisible bonds with every fiber of my being. The touch seared through my clothing and deep into my skin.

The unseen figure leaned in close behind me and stage-whispered in my ear with a deep, resonant voice of poisoned honey, "You picked the wrong team, Zack." I felt hot breath burning upon my ear and neck from above me, and caught a heady waft of what I can only describe as rotting peppermint and Polo cologne- which in spite of current circumstance seemed weird as hell.

Abaddon! It had to be. A thousand jibes came to mind and I wanted to hurl them and slash with my sword at the bastard - but a dark wave roiled over my spirit - a grim and horrifying antithesis to Amalek's gilded touch. The rapture, joy and hope of Amalek were swept away by a putrid roll of despondence and misery. The vile miasma emanated from Abaddon's heavy hand and nauseated me to my very bones.

The contents of my stomach surged upward involuntarily as if to escape the darkness invading my core and splattered Hiro's frozen form, my soul shrieking in abject horror.

I stiffened as tendrils of darkness lashed at me like razored spider webs, for the slightest moment thankful the unnatural binding kept my face passive and the bastard couldn't see the painful truth in my eyes. He soaked up my remembered pains like a desiccated vampire chomping on a hemophiliac fat chick, and my mind shamefully held droves of bitter fruit for him to harvest and gnaw on, and it just wouldn't stop. A host of rabid and barbed mealworms were tunneling through the marrow of my bones... over and over and over in a chittering feast of painful darkness.

Beth began to rise slowly from my arms, adding loss to the horror ripping through me. I tried shouting at the top of my lungs - tried vainly to will everything into motion again and again - but only heard the soft cackle of Abaddon and the sluggish thrumming of a pulse I prayed would just end.

Beth floated away towards the cave entrance, heavy drops of blood splashing across the red rock, each one a cacophony of sound in the unnatural silence, and tears ran down my motionless face.

"I want you to get used to this feeling, dog. I promise you it will be all you ever feel again."

A surge of viscous hate drowned out the misery engulfing me, threatening my consciousness with its ferocity. Abaddon's footfalls faded towards the cave entrance, and I stretched my eyes as far as they would go in an effort to catch even a glimpse of him, but the darkness and pain clouded any chance I might have. Tears clouded my peripheral vision, and all I managed to glimpse was a dark figure unhurriedly leaving the cave, the footfalls and snap of the cane a dirge to accompany the evil permeating my being.

I was alone with silent rage and whatever power that kept me fixed to the blood-covered cave floor, mentally screaming for Beth with whatever semblance of sanity I still held.

Chapter Twenty-One
Forgotten Promises

Director Salek entered Luna Base's vast Operations Center, a purposeful gait mirroring the determined look on his oddly disproportionate face. Conviction colored his oversized turquoise eyes, emotion only partially veiled by one who existed within and beyond a realm of time full humans simply could not comprehend. Frustration was an odd emotion rarely encountered by the placid director, but tendrils of it feathered his subconscious with a disconcerting tickle. Humanity's touch still thrummed strongly through his being, subtly tempering his convictions in spite of his expanded awareness.

The Sage-Maiden Angelicas had given him the names of the other Drakos on the Moon, and a kaleidoscope of possible outcomes streaked through his mind's eye. If he issued a certain command, then a pattern of events would unfold. Utter another and the wheels of fate would slip into another gear entirely, with even more possibilities spiraling out madly on infinite strings. Discerning all the possible outcomes had been the hallmark of his existence, shaping and following one of many paths shaped by the Creator. He had no other choice but to tread lightly, and carry a big, cosmic stick.

Sending the advance party of Tunaki had been a rather decisive slash with that staff of possibility, and the weave of time reflected it back to him in glaring, angry tones. Warnings from the source he'd not encountered before. A brazen deviation from the path his human side wanted to back ferociously - but nevertheless a detour from what could be.

There were filaments and threads shaping the possibilities that remained well beyond his scope of influence; all he could really do was sculpt as much possibility from within his own sphere - and hope for better lines of communication with those back on earth. The sky-skin continued to thwart all of the vast technological resources at his disposal, but he was not without some means of action.

The roulette wheel of possibility in his mind momentarily stopped turning, indicating a flashpoint of choice now open to his persuasion, but the possible pathways to achieve success were diminishing exponentially — and none of the paths were without immense suffering, bloodshed and loss. However, none were as dire if he failed to attempt anything at all.

He spoke, weeping inwardly at a choice among none, but nevertheless must be taken if anything were to ever be right again. Deception spewed forth from his mouth as easy as if he'd been speaking it forever.

For the first and only time in an existence that defied time, Salek lied to those he was charged with protecting - defying his creator, his own sense of justice and all that was *right* - and the universe became a slightly darker space.

****

I'd been immobilized for what I guessed to be about eight hours before the world once again shifted back into motion. At least I think it was eight hours; time is hard to judge when you go from panic to freak to calm in an ongoing, vicious cycle - all while being simmered in a crockpot of demonic bouillabaisse.

I hated the immobility - always had. A cousin had tied me up in a big quilt when I was five, the only time in memory I recalled being truly terrified until Dad untied the knots and knocked cousin Brad upside the head. But Brad hadn't plunged me into a hateful darkness - just fear.

The time shackled in Abaddon's grip was the first time in days I'd been able to think - even amidst the maelstrom of putrid influence; I guess I owed the dark bastard a favor for that small grace. Things had started to click - in spite of the blackness, giving me the impression I might finally have a grip on what I needed to do. Tenuous, at best - but it was something.

Hiro slid ungracefully in the now fully congealed pool of Kilkenor and human blood at my knees, a stunned expression on his wizened face as he slammed into my chest, the remnants of my breakfast coating him, while the din of reality moving back into motion roared into my ears.

"What the hell?" he stammered, looking around quickly to try and spot where Beth had vanished off to, or who had blown chunks all over him.

I caught him, then began to roll stiffened neck and back muscles that felt as though I'd been lifting weights for days without rest. I flexed my jaw muscles and began hopping — just because I could.

"Abaddon's got her, Hiro - and the bastard is long gone." Hiro looked at me like I'd lost my last marble, and when I tried to explain what had happened, the questioning look only grew more skeptical. The lingering touch of evil probably didn't help my case, but Hiro seemed as non-plussed as could be expected.

"I guess I really shouldn't be surprised," he said, his stoic face a deadpan calm. "You roll out for a talking storm and now there's Wookies riding white stallions on the front porch - kicking the shit out of monsters Wes Craven couldn't dream up... an evil deity popping in to say 'howdy' and stopping time seems to fit rather nicely into this acid-trip gone waaaaay bad... you reckon we can track the sum' bitch?"

Jacob trotted over to where Hiro and I were huddled and Hiro eyed the big Cytheran with a disbelieving gaze. "Now I know I'm tripping hard - Professor Watkins? Ain't no way in hell...."

Jacob looked at Hiro for a long moment then clarity dawned on his face, *and a bit of alarm?* - and he extended a blood-caked hand to the wiry Texan. "Nice to see you with your eyes open for a change, Mr. Masamune. I haven't been called 'Professor' in a very long time - 'Jacob' will be sufficient, sir." Hiro remained silently perplexed and limply shook the proffered hand with his mouth agape while Jacob focused his attention back to me.

"I saw the one you called Beth taken, along with three other young females; the remaining living Kilkenor in the cave have also gone - no doubt by some dark means Abaddon wields - but the dead remain and we can harvest their bloodstones and see what the Sage Maiden may garner before..."

"...Not all of them are gone," I interrupted, running for the cave entrance, the others quickly following.

It was invigorating to get out from the confined space of the cave. I breathed in several welcome gasps of freer air, visibly shaking free from the taint of Abaddon's touch, then let my gaze fall upon a series of darker shadows my senses had been drawn to - although I wasn't exactly sure about what or how my senses were being guided.

This didn't feel like Amalek's or Abaddon's touch, it seemed somehow inherent to me - perhaps my body awaking to the further changes Jacob had briefly alluded to. Could my dance with darkness have brought about some sort of transition?

There were whispers and tendrils of variegated "thingies" in my field of vision, and they didn't seem to fade when I closed my eyes - sort of like the afterimage a rather brilliant flashbulb might leave behind, but fixed in intensity with every shadow and hue captured in crisp relief, along with something my regular eyes told me shouldn't be there, but my Liland-affected eyes seemed to soak up greedily, like welcome shade in July.

The humans, Cytherans and Tunaki surrounding me emitted varying levels of a muted light from the center of their foreheads that pulsed in time with their respective heartbeats. Each glow seemed to emit the signature of its bearer, a unique emission like a fingerprint or snowflake, with hue and intensity subtly delineating one from the other. The Tunaki pulsed in shades of red, the Cytheran an almost canary yellow, and the humans looked more like prism light.

I could seemingly adjust how much of this light I saw with simple concentration, but the dark void being projected from the six Kilkenor took all of my immediate attention. Brizzock, Curtz and Taka were standing in front of a massive Kilkenor, looking like linebackers waiting for a running back to bust through the line, Mouse pacing like a midget alley cat behind them, covered from head to toe in sticky blue - and all their clear blades dripping with the pungent Kilkenor blood, feral grins splayed across confident faces as they bounced lithely on ginger feet.

I could sense what the Kilkenor, Tunaki and Mouse were going to do three heart-beats before they did it — my confinement had brought that realization to life when I thought back to slaying the six Kilkenor before I met Abaddon — I *knew* what they were going to do before they did. Otherwise I would have been a smashed hamburger patty on the side of Thunder Mountain.

As one, Brizzock and Curtz leapt into the air to the right and left of the beast with an agility defying their stature, their blades a blur cleanly severing both arms off the surprised fiend, while at the same time Taka leapt straight up in the air, scissor-kicking his tree-trunk legs and bellowing a guttural roar that rang deep in my chest. Mouse shot straight forward beneath him, deftly shoving his new blade straight up beneath the Kilkenor's sternum all the way to the hilt, while Taka sliced it's head off cleanly. Ballerinas didn't have as much grace as that unlikely quartet did - you'd think they'd been hunting Kilkenor together for years.

The remaining five beasts fell under a fusillade of other Tunaki blades, their black essences slipping into the dust like enchanted mist, and I let my gaze drift off to the south towards more pressing concerns. Abaddon had Beth - and what I guessed to be Smokey's granddaughters - and I shuddered at what he could and would do to them. I'd only glimpsed his evil, and it had driven me close to madness. I stabbed my blade into the skull of the dead kilkenor at my feet and heard a gratifying sizzle as it boiled away to nothing - a violet hue emanating from the blade as it banished black tendrils into sulfury vapor. Part of me craved to hear that hiss again and again, and I knew I would somehow get more than I could possibly handle.

Chapter Twenty-Two
Stairwell to Purgatory

Beth lazed on the king-size bed, tucked in between no less than half a dozen pillows, one bare leg peeking out from the cream-colored, silk sheet draped across her. She sipped on her second Mimosa of the morning, idly nibbling on a chocolate-covered strawberry from the fruit-laden silver platter beside her. A sated, languid calm enveloped her, as gentle as the temperate, slightly salty breeze drifting through the open window, lazily stirring the sheer drapes in a slow dance of tranquil perfection that mirrored her own peace. Seabird's trilled a southern lullaby from the skies over the mouth of the Savannah River; far enough away that she had to wonder if they were singing from the Georgia or South Carolina side, and she smiled knowing that was the only question she had to ponder today - and whatever the answer would be, she'd still be happy.

She heard the shower running in the bathroom, her husband Mark singing a Beach Boys tune way-off key as only he could — the seabirds might've been sweeter on the ears, but they didn't make her smile the way he did, and he'd given her multiple reasons to smile since well before the sun peeked its head above the coast this morning.

He'd truly shocked her the night before - not an easy feat after a decade of marriage - but nevertheless a delightful surprise. He told her that his early retirement package from the Marines was approved, and since she had been summarily drummed out of the space program, it was time for the both of them to begin the family they'd dreamed about years ago.

The Air Force wanted to transfer her to the Academy in Colorado Springs - teaching ethics to aspiring officers, a position she'd secretly craved for years if the reaches of space seemed out of reach - and they'd bought a cabin in the black forest region three years ago, just a quick jaunt away from the Academy grounds. *Life really couldn't get any better,* she thought. *Almost as if I planned it this way.*

The fact that she couldn't bear children was a hurdle they'd overcome long ago, both fully engrossed in their military careers. Hell, the fact that they had enough time for each other was a feat in itself- juggling challenging billets between two different services had been a miracle. Now he'd arranged for the adoption they'd both dreamed about for years. She was going to be a mother - and that was all that mattered... wasn't it?

A tiny hint of misgiving still reared its ugly head in the back of her mind. She'd always been fiercely independent - there was simply no way a woman in this day and age could clamber for her own role in this supposed man's world without it - but she still felt a longing to continue forging her *own* path. Plus, there was something else just beyond reach of her thoughts that seemed to slip away, something she was missing - but what it was she couldn't put her fingers on.

The salt breeze and discord of her husband's song banished the doubts in a smother of comfort - and she stuffed her fears away as golden sunshine wafted into the luxury suite. Why did it seem like such a long time since she'd seen the sun?

This afternoon she would meet the child that would be hers. Mark had warned her that the child would be different... *challenged* he'd said - but they'd overcome so much together, and there were so many children with special needs that needed good homes. Like Mark said - even if the child seemed beastly and foreign — that statement had alarmed her a bit — it would nevertheless be theirs to raise, and theirs to shape - no matter how different it seemed to the rest of the world.

No matter how different...no matter.

The message light on the phone beside the bed began flashing in an iridescent shade of purple - *strange, I never heard it ring.*

She picked up the phone but before she could put it to her ear the tiny speaker screamed like a thousand banshees in flight, and the receiver transformed into a writhing black snake in her hand - her grip just below the serpent's neck, sickly-yellow venom dripping from bared fangs that easily sank deep into the soft flesh of her wrist. She tried to fling the snake off, but it held fast like a tightened vise, its muscled body wrapping around her forearm as she shook violently, sending the platter of strawberries skittering across the silken sheets.

Venom spread like fire through her upper body, and before darkness carried her away into oblivion she swore she heard Zack Dalton screaming out her name, and idly wondered why she would hear him of all people.

****

Strategos Andrex and Jacob stood with me at the base of the Buddhist Stupa below Thunder Mountain - West Sedona laid out in a sprawl before us, the once pristine horizon pock-marked with fingers of ugly black smoke chasing the purple, darkening sky. Nightfall was fast approaching.

Tracking the kilkenor wouldn't be a problem - they left a trail even a deaf and blind city-slicker could follow. The greasy smell of burning corpses and rot carried on the breeze, but Andrex was more focused on my sword in his hands. He'd been pawing it since he saw the Kilkenor skull sizzle beneath its tip, caressing it like a newborn babe.

He hummed a barely audible single note so low in pitch that I felt it more than heard it, while gently running two fingers the size of bratwursts up and down the blade. The red aura emanating from his forehead shimmered in a vibrating pulse that seemed to match his tone, and faint tendrils of violet flowed from the sword through his fingers, up his arm and into the red pulse, as if he was communing with my blade on a spiritual level.

"*Bemoroh AuOmonea de Kharashuotoa, Bikiapoa t-yo deam bhodea Bikhab, Zack Dalton,*" he said, the lyrical Tunaki-Aramaic rolling off his tongue like silken sandpaper. "Master Craftsman of Magic, Stone is with this one," my mind translated at once - still blown away that I possessed such an amazing skill.

"I would know more of this blade's construction, Zack Dalton, this *Liland* you speak of from your sky-skin is greater than you may know." He handed me the blade back hilt-first, nodding

115

in appreciation. "You toppers continue to impress - you've come a long way since my time. Were that the Tunaki and Cytherans had done likewise..." He shot Jacob a cool gaze, but Jacob was too busy intently scanning the sky to the south to notice - or he was a lot better under Tunaki reproach than I would be.

Hiro was approaching us with Mouse and his deadly trio of Tunaki after harvesting all of the bloodstones they could find for Angelicas. So far the only thing the Sage Maiden could determine was that the bad guys were heading south toward some great pit - and there were more kilkenor scattered throughout the region. Thousands, she'd said - and likely more to come.

Smokey and a few other men I didn't recognize trailed a little farther behind - all of them human with rifles slung at their shoulders, and all of them a bit wary of the Tunaki and Kenawak- in spite of having seen them in action against the formidable Kilkenor. *Men could be some pretty close-minded dumb-asses more often than not. We'd best keep a close eye on the newcomers.*

The horses and Kenawak grazed nearby on small patches of clumped desert grass, Smokey's grandsons fawning over the Kenawak and Cytheran mounts, scrubbing their coats clean of kilkenor blood and gore, and singing what I guessed to be a Hopi song. The melody was haunting and dissonant to my western ears, but the animals seemed to find comfort in the ancient tune, and took to the boys like old friends.

"To quote the great Ricky Ricardo, I think you got some 'splaining to do, Zack - starting with just what the hell are we supposed to do now?" said Hiro, plopping down on the concrete base surrounding the stupa, absently scratching at his nether regions, his bravado seemingly restored back to banty rooster status.

"What makes you think I've got a clue, Hiro?"

He finished scratching himself and pointed in the general direction of Mouse and his entourage of furry killers.

"Your genius buddy over there with the sweet diamond blade told us all about your encounter with the glowing friend of Zeus's. I reckon you been touched by the Olympians themselves. In any book I'd say that puts your happy ass in charge." He smiled playfully and went back to scratching at whatever ailed his crotch - until Angelicas approached from the eastern path with two Tunaki warriors. Some things you just don't do in front of a lady - no matter the species.

Smokey drew close with the other men, looking haggard and bone-weary, no doubt feeling the loss of his progeny, but there was a flint in his eyes of hunger for the ones who caused the pain. Age doesn't seem to dampen a thirst for retribution.

"Major Dalton, I'd like to introduce you to the men responsible for helping you kick a lot of Kilkenor ass today" said Smokey, motioning to the armed men surrounding him, "This is Master Gunnery-Sergeant Eddie Killmore, his son Corporal Troy Killmore and a few of the more scruffy members of the ragtag Sedona Volunteer Militia."

The Master Guns was a walking recruiting poster for the old-school Marine Corps. And how could you not love a jarhead with that last name? *Killmore - I bet their drill instructors loved the hell out of that.* He stood at least 6' 5, easily hefting 280 pounds with smooth features chiseled out of ebony granite. His skin was the color of fine espresso, his son a carbon copy of the father, though touched with a faint dose of cream, and both with the hard eyes of hungry warriors who just endured an all you can eat buffet of whoop-ass, yet were cautiously ready for seconds.

The Master Guns sized me up as only a Senior Non-Commissioned Officer could, no doubt wondering why a Marine Major was wearing a kilt and a sword while sporting purple peepers - not exactly the uniform of the day as proscribed by the Commandant - no matter the circumstance.

"Nice to see a fellow Belleau Woodsman in the midst of all this chaos, Master Guns - and damn fine shooting," I said, "You both still active duty by chance - whatever that means these days..."

"Yes, sir - you might say that, although neither one of us have seen a paycheck in awhile. I was on terminal leave awaiting retirement, camping way off the grid north of here with my son when all the stuff associated with Halcyon went down. We holed up with Smokey when the nukes started flying, and haven't been able to establish contact with anybody wearing a uniform since. I guess we're a couple squared away jarheads that happen to be UA (Unauthorized Absence) due to circumstances beyond anybody's control."

I nodded to the Master Guns in understanding and pointed to the obviously non-military men he had with him. They looked like they knew their way around the woods - but didn't have the disciplined air of those who'd stood on the yellow footprints of the recruit training depots at Parris Island and San Diego.

"More circumstance, sir - Sedona looked like Dodge City on free whiskey day for awhile after the radiation dissipated. Local law enforcement was nowhere to be seen, no Reserve or National Guard troops. My son and I sort of put together this group to try and keep the peace with all the refugees flocking to the red rocks. These men were mostly jeep-tour drivers, and represent half of our local defense group. We were just checking in on Smokey and Hiro when those fucked up scorpion things showed up - I met Major Hodgson and she briefed me on your story..." He balked a bit and I chuckled slightly, "...she didn't mention the big fuzzy guys or the Clydesdales on steroids though, sir, although I was damn glad to see you all show up, for what it's worth..."

He hesitated and looked over at Strategos Andrex like a surprised thief coming face-to-face with a pissed off pit bull in a darkened back yard.

"...I'm not sure how appropriate this will be, sir - but these men have families in Sedona they'd like to check on as soon as possible - any way some of these *Tunaki* could be persuaded to join us for a look-see?" I looked to Jacob and he translated the request to Andrex who nodded quickly, then barked an order for the Tunaki to mount up.

"Time to dance, Master Guns - let's go check on your people... *it'll give me some time to figure out just what the hell we need to do next.*"

****

Even the grim touch of Abaddon did little to prepare me for what I discovered when we entered Sedona. Bodies - or what was left of them, lay in viscous piles on every sidewalk and storefront. The few trees along the main thoroughfare held dismembered human remains within their branches, as if flung there by some powerful, shredding centrifuge.

Killmore's militiamen looked ashen and hurried off in groups of two and three with Tunaki warriors shadowing them to different parts of the town - threading their way through patchwork tents that seemed to occupy every bit of free space across the landscape. No amount of optimism would let me think they'd be returning wearing smiles. The very air smelled devoid of life and hope.

The Kilkenor had obviously waded through here with a much larger force than we'd faced on the mountain, no way the locals could've stood up to the assault, even if Killmore and crew had been present.

Abaddon wanted me to see this. The fucker spared me just so I could get a glimpse of his power.

The big Marine was mounted on a Tennessee Walker and led Andrex, Jacob, Hiro and me to a strip mall just beyond the river. I remembered the place from my visit here years ago with my wife. We'd enjoyed a few pints and laughter with some hippy locals at a little Irish pub called Mooney's and watched amazing sunsets painting the red rocks to the west.

That seemed so freaking long ago and a world away.

I held the memory close inside like a cherished love letter, idly hoping the place was still open for business. A pint or nine of Mooney's Irish Red seemed to be just what I needed.

Master Guns dismounted in front of the bar, the former glass front doors replaced with ¼ inch plates of welded steel - decoratively embellished with a four leaf clover etched in acid. Guess the place was still open - just not as accessible as it used to be.

Master Guns Killmore unslung his deer rifle and rapped out shave-and-a-haircut with the butt end of the rifle across the thick plate, a gap in the steel just above eye level quickly sliding open to reveal a pair of obviously terrified hazel eyes.

"It's me and some friends, Nick - open up, okay? And don't freak out about the big guy - I swear he's on our side."

The sound of sliding steel and chains carried through the massive door, then opened on well-oiled hinges to reveal the owner I'd met years before - although he'd been smiling warmly back then instead of looking horrified beyond belief.

"Jesus Christ, Eddie - what the hell is going on? What the fuck were those things? Did you see what they did to the women? It's friggin' apoc — " Nick froze in mid-sentence as he took in the form of Andrex, his face paling enough that I thought he might piss himself or pass out - maybe both.

"Andrex has that effect on a lot of people, Nick. He's a Tunaki - I'll explain everything to you over a pint if you've got any. Zack Dalton. We met the first month you opened the place," Nick absently took my hand but never took his eyes off Andrex, his mouth wide open.

119

"Breathe dude, breathe," Eddie said, "Let us in and tell us what went down. The big guy is definitely on our side, okay?"

Eddie's calming bass seemed to bring the bar owner back to earth, and he motioned us all in - quickly shutting the door behind us - but giving Andrex a wide berth and still looking pale as skimmed milk.

The place hadn't changed much since I'd last been there, although the shelves weren't quite as well-stocked as they'd once been, and two massive copper stills stood in the small alcove where the dart players and regulars hung out. A wall of signed dollar bills framed the bar, the one Laura and I signed still tucked up proud in the top-left corner. Seeing her flowing script and the oversized smiley face and rocket she'd crafted made me smile.

We bellied up to the bar - Hiro rubbing his hands and grinning like we were on a weekend poker run instead of having just rode through the streets of hell. *Dude must really need a beer.* Andrex remained standing, the barstools no match for his massive frame, the roof brushing his massive head even stooped, but he leaned down on the bar with his palms flat - I swear I heard the wood creak. He took in the surroundings with a keen intent, sniffing the air appreciably.

"Is this the headquarters of Killmore's local army, Zack Dalton?" said Andrex, his deep Tunaki voice booming in the small tavern - and this time I think Nick really did piss himself.

I noticed the aura of the men with me when Andrex spoke, and saw how their essence seemed to repel his red flow - except for Hiro. A few wisps of red seemed to slip into Hiro's 'stream' of shifting hues of white light - and I understood why immediately.

I ignored Andrex' question and asked Hiro what he thought the Tunaki had said. Hiro looked a bit puzzled, but replied "Not much, Zack - something about Killmore's head - or where he keeps it," he shot Jacob a hard look and pointed an accusing finger - "Like I said, it's been a helluva long time since I was in seminary in *his* class - I've slept since then, young man."

"I want to try something, Hiro - and it might be a little weird," I said. "Andrex, do me a favor and start talking - it doesn't matter what you say as long as it makes sense - I want to see if I can get others to understand Tunaki the same way Amalek did for me and Director Salek did for Mouse." He nodded and began droning on about the surroundings, picking things at random and describing them in detail.

120

The red hues still seemed to bounce back from the humans - with that occasional snippet of understanding slipping through Hiro's aura. I reached out to touch Hiro and he backed up a bit giving me a wary glare. "Relax, Hiro - I think I know what I'm doing."

I could sense the essence of Hiro, and when I touched him it came at me in a clarity of brilliance and understanding. Andrex continued to speak, and I saw and felt the waves that would make Hiro capable of 'receiving' what Andrex was saying.

If I touch him right - there - and shift this - here...

Hiro's flows began to run brighter with the red Tunaki hues as I coaxed his essence into understanding, and his eyes opened wide and he stared at Andrex, dumbfounded. "Holy Shit - I just understood everything he said! Where were you in 1958, Zack - I could've got out of taking Professor Watkins' whole damn class!"

I laughed along with him - and sensed an oddly genuine hostility and distaste from Hiro towards Jacob - *it can wait - don't intrude* - the others looked puzzled, and I filed the thought away for later, while Andrex described the miniature garnish skewers in finite detail - "... the miniature swords are in bright colors of red, green and yellow - perhaps for cleaning of tiny Topper teeth or for marking out battle plans upon a map..."

I motioned for Nick to come closer, smiled and laid my hand on his forearm, and grasped Andrex's arm, "Listen to him, Nick," I said and had their flows in sync in under three heartbeats, then did the same for Eddie in short order.

My joy in discovering just a fraction of what I could now do was short-lived, snuffing out as soon as Nick began describing what he'd seen, and others began returning from their searches bearing equally grim accounts.

Chapter Twenty-Three
Pinhole to Hades

Isabella wanted Scary Lizard Man to go away.

He didn't look at her the same way the nice man dressed up like a character from *Braveheart* did.

Her brother Enrico loved *Braveheart* — Isabella only watched the parts with the French Princess - so she could see all the beautiful dresses and the pretty ribbons and braids in the Princess' hair; otherwise it was full of *boy* stuff. Swords and blood and a lot of yelling. Enrico said the men in the movie were brave and fought for freedom - maybe the nice man would help her get home - free from the scary Lizard people and Scorpion monsters and big hairy Monkey monsters - if that's what freedom meant, anyways.

But Braveheart Man couldn't help Enrico, the Scorpion monsters killed him when they took Isabella and Mommy away.

Isabella didn't want to think about that.

Braveheart Man said they'd all get to see their Mommies real soon, then go home, but the little boy holding Isabella's hand - the only boy - must not have believed it because he kept crying loudly, rubbing his nose on the sleeve of the soft white robe all of the children now wore; his soft golden curls bouncing with each rapid sniffle.

Isabella liked her white robe. It was pretty and smelled like flowers and was as soft as the belly of her cat Mister Binx, not itchy like the sweater GrandPa Smokey gave her when she turned five just a few days ago. Braveheart Man and Monkey Lady had given them the robes after a long, hot bath in a giant tub carved out of red rock that looked like GrandPa Smokey's cave house.

Monkey Lady rubbed tingly lotion on all their tummies that smelled like cough syrup, the red kind that tasted like cherries. She wished her and Mommy had stayed at the cave instead of going to Grasshopper Point to throw rocks - but that shouldn't matter since she'd soon get to see her Mommy and go home.

Monkey lady stood behind them and herded them down a long, wide corridor lit by pretty lamps the same blue color of her Aunt Lisa's favorite earrings. The lizard man was far in front, his green and gold robes shimmering silently in the soft light, but there was still the screaming and wails of women coming from somewhere and everywhere. Always the screaming that never stopped, and it was getting louder. Braveheart Man and Big Monkey Man were following, Big Monkey Man looking back with an ugly face and laughing.

The little boy gripped Isabella's hand tighter, almost hurting her but she pulled him along with the group, a brighter light ahead opening up into what looked to be a vast room.

Maybe this was where they would get to see their Mommies. Isabella couldn't wait to show her the new robe, and her tummy was starting to get really hot from Monkey Lady's lotion.

They exited the smooth tunnel into a wide open field, and Isabella learned where all the screaming came from.

Mommies were nailed naked to X-shaped crosses everywhere Isabella looked, and their cries swelled when the little ones came into view. More lizard people scurried about on all fours, but they weren't green and brown like Scary Lizard Man. They had people skin in all colors, and people hair and private parts - but on a lizard body with mean yellow eyes like Mister Binx before he would bite you.

The naked Lizard People all turned and sniffed the air when the group approached the field, but some of them were standing in front of the Mommies doing what Isabella once saw the man from Circle K doing with Aunt Lisa behind the grocery store.

Scary Lizard Man swooped into the group quicker than Isabella could blink and snatched the little boy up by his neck with one brightly polished, four-fingered claw. The little boy was silent but shook violently, and had an accident on the shiny robes of Lizard Man, who didn't seem to notice or care. Lizard Man sniffed at the little boy's tummy, and saliva dripped from razor sharp teeth as it made a sound like Mister Binx when you rubbed his back. But way louder and way scarier.

A sticky, red wetness blinded Isabella as something hot spread across her face. She tried to wipe the hot goo from her eyes and saw through a red mist her beautiful robe splattered with blood and gore, then saw Scary Lizard Man throw what was left of the little boy over his shoulder to the Lizard People behind him, some of what Isabella guessed was the little boy's inside parts clinging to Lizard Man's teeth like overlong strips of oily, raw bacon. He licked razor sharp teeth with a thick, barbed tongue and cruel, slanted eyes of radiant yellow mocked Isabella and the others, then hissed louder than Mister Binx did when Enrico held him by the tail.

"Take them to their bitches, Brood! My new children grow hungry!" it roared, and Isabella tried to slip away to a happy place in her mind.

The people-skinned lizards swarmed into the children like a pack of zombie wolves; clicking, snarling and whisking them away in human-like, webbed hands bristling with broad, flat claws and razor-thin little hairs across the back of their hands and arms; shaded in rows like pristine, porcupine needles.

Time stopped for Isabella as the cream-colored Lizard man stretched her out in front of him like a corn on the cob, one massive hand under her chin, the other grasping both her legs and pulling as if to slowly rip her apart, sniffing roughly and long at her tummy, saliva gushing from his mouth in a hissy spray as it raised its long-bridged, flat snout to the air, hunting for the kindred scent and bellowing when it caught it.

Isabella again feebly tried to slip into a realm beyond fear and touch as the lizard man darted off on two legs quickly through the sea of crucifixion, scrambling in a steady gait like the chimpanzees she saw on one of her animal DVD's.

Isabella knew she wasn't going home, but Isabella was already far away from this scary place that couldn't be real. She saw Braveheart Man laughing with Big Monkey Man, and she hoped Scary Lizard Man would eat him, too - and Monkey Lady.

Mommies that didn't hang limply from the backward tilted, railroad-tie crosses cried out as Isabella and the lizard man sped by. All the Mommies had giant swollen bellies that wiggled under blood-caked skin, pulled so tight it looked like they would pop at the slightest touch. Their screams were only a distant sound to

Isabella now, her placid face immune to the surreal horrors around her.

The monster came to a stop and viciously twisted her to face forward, releasing one claw to let her dangle inches in front of her mother's beaten and bloody face. Her mother didn't cry out like the others, and a warmth flooded Isabella's soul as she lost herself in her Mommy's strong eyes. Isabella was pulled back and the beast stabbed a claw precisely above her Mommy's bulging tummy and between her greatly swollen breasts. Fluid and blood escaped in a little fountain, ignored by Isabella who remained rapt in her Mommy's unwavering stare, glistening pink heads beginning to emerge in a writhing slither of steaming twitters and hungry cries, beneath her and yet a world away.

"Drakos Basmakka Bealmaa!! Drakos Feast Forever!!" shouted the beasts as one, holding each of the children above the squirming abominations springing to life, Isabella somewhere in the farthest reaches of her mind feeling an abrupt sting and tug as the monster rent the little girl's tummy open, hatchlings leaping upward to their first taste of flesh... Isabella felt sad for the poor little girl, but there was nothing she could do for her now... it was time for her and Mommy to go home.

Chapter Twenty-Four
Closed Doors

I sat outside of Mooney's on the patio where Lisa and I had once enjoyed those fabulous sunsets, puffing on a halfway decent cigar Eddie Killmore had scrounged up. I thought of Doc Vandenberg and the last stogie I'd enjoyed a harsh reality ago, then eyed the underside of the darkening sky-skin, wondering if reality would ever again resemble what I once knew. Muffled Tunaki and human conversation drifted from the bar, floating Hiro and Eddie along to my table, Hiro clutching a new pitcher of sky juice and an overfilled pewter tankard. They sat down with me not saying a word, no doubt lost in their own musings of the grim tales told to us by the survivors of the day's horrifying events.

We sat in companionable silence as the darkness deepened, the wispy lines in the sky-skin disappearing in the gloom, Nick wandering out to light the few oil lamps and tiki torches framing the patio. No breeze stirred the flames, and Sedona seemed as quiet as a morgue at midnight.

Brizzock silently appeared from the gloom of the parking lot, his scarred Tunaki features looking slightly alarmed as he paused, gave me a curt nod, then entered the bar, returning a brief moment later with Andrex - who looked equally concerned, and a little pissed.

"Where is the Cytheran Jacob?" asked Andrex, a hard edge to his eyes.

I motioned towards the trees framing the southern parking

lot, "He wandered off that way with the Cytheran messenger who arrived earlier - maybe twenty or thirty minutes ago. I thought he was going to relieve himself, but he has been gone awhile now that you mention it. What gives?" I looked to where the horses were tied, and noticed Jacob's mount was no longer there, it had to have been moved before I even came outside.

"I told you that sumbitch was no good," accused Hiro, wiping a violet froth from his upper lip. "What'd he do?"

"Tenegress Prime is closed, Zack Dalton - our way into Redstone has been blocked. Brizzock's scouts have attempted the other gateways, but they are likewise closed - this can only be done from the inside - and only by order of the Cytheran and Tunaki leadership." Andrex eyed Hiro curiously. "Why do you question the Cytheran leader, blacksmith?"

Hiro drained his tankard and began immediately refilling it from the glass pitcher, his face a mask of frustration and long forgotten fears.

"Back in the 50's when I was in seminary in northern California and the man you call 'Jacob' was my Aramaic professor - there was a lot of weird shit going down. We had stables, a lot of farm animals and fields we tended as part of the school - then critters started disappearing or showing up mutilated real bad, like they was gnawed on by some nasty predator none of us had ever seen.," He took a plaintive sip from his tankard, not bothering to wipe the froth from his upper lip and continued in his languid, west Texas drawl.

"This old boy Jenkins - an army vet who'd fought in WWII and Korea - well, he and I snuck off one night and grabbed us some beers and whiskey and were drinking behind the old hen house... Jenkins got this far away look in his eyes, talking about some of the horrors he'd seen in Europe and Korea. Then he told me to stay away from Professor Watkins - said the man was 'evil beyond anything he'd ever seen in the wars', and that he knew 'first-hand' that the professor was party to what was happening to the animals." He took another swig and eyed all of us seriously. "You boys know when liquor starts flowing it's hard for a good man to lie to you - and I never doubted what old Jenkins said about your Jacob." He set his mug down and nodded, obviously finished with his tale.

"If Jacob is so evil - then why would Amalek have touched him - like he did me?" I asked.

127

"Because Amalek is an idealistic fool that is easily duped," came a deep, commanding voice from the darkened parking lot, those of us at the table rising quickly, the sound of swords and pistols clearing hilts and holsters overshadowed by multiple, booted footfalls steadily approaching across the asphalt.

"Time has done little to improve your ugly face, Strategos - but Stone keep you, nevertheless," boomed a voice tailor-made to ring clearly across the din of ancient battlefields. Andrex motioned for us to safe our weapons, and I warily obliged as a towering, red-bearded figure emerged from the shadows into the torchlight, flanked by three serious looking henchmen. The speaker was only slightly taller than myself, with forearms like anvils gauntleted in thick, bronze-studded, brown leather. His aura rang a brilliant white to my 'other' eyes, like a human but much more vibrant and intense - more pure, perhaps. A long mane of unkempt auburn and red curls framed a serious face that looked to have been on the receiving end of many blows, sheltering piercing blue eyes that spoke of humor, kindness and unabashed intensity. A breastplate of boiled leather covered an impressive chest, with a gilded celtic cross emblazoned across it. A long cloak of a deep, forest green draped solid shoulders, clasped around his neck with a golden chain that would make a rap artist drool with envy.

"You never were good at seeing Tunaki beauty, Eindridi - and my nose tells me you still smell like a dirty goat's balls." I could hear the laughter and warmth in Andrex's voice. He clasped the newcomers extended forearm in a grasp that would've ripped my own from my shoulders. Eindridi's cohorts looked like extras from a Conan the Barbarian film, and remained behind their leader with stolid, unmoving faces. "Stone keep you, Eindridi - sit and drink - if you are here, then there truly is madness afoot and the last battle fast approaches."

Nick emerged from the bar with more tankards and pitchers, and we began to shuffle the tables around to make room for everyone to sit. The henchmen didn't sit, instead quickly pounding a tankard of sky juice, then fading back into the darkness with a nod from their leader. Eindridi laid a massive, formidable hammer on the table in front of him, showered Nick's tray with a huge pile of gold coins, and Hiro began laughing hysterically, tears streaming from his eyes. All of us eyed the old metal worker curiously - wondering what was so funny, or if the old man had finally lost his last marble. Hiro stood and raised his tankard high in salute to the newcomer, drawing in deep breaths to maintain his control, then eyed Eddie and I with a mischievous twinkle in his eyes. "You boys really don't have a fucking clue, do you? I know education has taken a pretty good nose-dive over the years - and maybe I'm just a sucker for ancient mythology - but even I know that Eindridi is just one of the names this fellow goes by. How's about Asabrag, Ennilang, Rym or Sonnung? Ringing any bells?" Eindridi raised his eyebrows in surprise, smiled at Hiro and clanked his tankard with Hiro's, Eddie and I still staring in perplexed confusion as Hiro cackled louder and danced in place like a giddy school boy. "Thor!! You dumbass jarheads!! Heard of that one, maybe? You're drinking beer with the God of Thunder himself!! Fucking Thor!! If that don't beat all - Smokey's gonna shit! If I'm dreaming don't wake me, cause this is one helluva ride!" He continued his one-man happy dance and Eddie and I stared at Endridi - Thor - in disbelief - and awe.

"So you've heard of me," said the God of Thunder, sending Hiro into another fit of raucous laughter, which he chased with a long draw on his tankard, finally collapsing into his seat, smiling bigger than any man ever had a right to.

Aliens, Bigfoot, ancient Gods, reptilian monsters - and now drinking sky-juice with freaking Norse legends. I rubbed the pocket where I kept my package of peanut M&M's, my last link to normal, then looked up at the faint whisper of the moon drifting palely beyond the sky-skin. I lifted my tankard to the heavens and toasted silently, *Wish you were here for this one, Doc - its really starting to get interesting... here's to the luckiest friggin' co-pilot on the planet.*

Cheers, Doc.

**** End of Episode I ****

129

Author's Note:

Cliffhangers suck - but you gotta do what you gotta do.
Just getting to this point has been a long and uphill battle, and it never would have seen the light of day without the assistance of my friends and family.

Special thanks to my wife for encouraging me to continue with the tale when I thought it was dead. You rock, babe - even when our life plays out like a bad country song

Huge kudos to those who took the time to wade through chapters when nobody else would, with special nods to Eddie Kaddi, Andre Tatum, Terry Fedric, Angie Perrigo, Jason Hall and Tom Bielski.

Most special thanks to Editor Eric Maywar, and to Brad Crandall for hooking us up.

Sandra Sofia Johnson brought Halcyon to life with her beautiful artwork. All those hands in every chapter heading, and the Drakos on the cover are her awesome creation! Thank you!

If all goes as planned - and it seldom does - Halcyon's Wake will consist of at least three episodes. I hope you've enjoyed the beginning of this tale - be sure and tell me all about it. Much love and peace to you and yours! The biggest thank you goes out to you, no book is worth a hoot without loyal readers.

May Stone Keep You.

-A Dale Triplett
Laveen, Arizona
April 2016

About the Author

Arbra Dale Triplett is an author, journalist, copywriter, veteran and editor. He's been writing fiction, advertising, marketing and UFO-related content for almost twenty years. Born in Springfield, Missouri to an Air Force family, he grew up in Texas, Colorado and Illinois before spending thirteen years in Germany. He studied English and History at Oklahoma Christian University, Harding University and Lubbock Christian. He served abroad in the Marine Corps for 4 years, drove semi trucks from coast to coast hauling anything from live bees to oversized freight, and flew in the Air Force as a Loadmaster on a C-130 cargo transport. He's hung his hat from Alaska to Florida and a lot of places in between. You'll find him every year at the UFO Congress in Arizona, soaking up conversation at the fire pit with a cold beverage at hand. He and his wife hang their hat in the west valley of Phoenix, Arizona. For more information visit www.daletriplett.com. Follow Dale on Twitter @DaleTriplett and visit The Halcyon's Wake Chronicles Fan Page on Facebook

A sneak peek of what's coming up in Episode II…

Halcyon's Wake: Love

Episode II
of
The Halcyon's Wake Chronicles

Prologue

Elaina wound her way down the hidden stairwell carved near the access point of Tenegress Omega, a silken cloth covering her face to help mask the putrid and sour stench of the human captives... and other things... wafting upward through the spiral corridor. She was far enough away to not hear the screams - thankfully - but she knew the scent would likely never leave her again, if only lingering in the imagination of her conscious and nightmares. Pity, she thought. It had taken her months to find the perfect shade of complimentary pink thistle-silks for her lavish floor-length gown.

Jacob was a fool, of that she was now firmly convinced; but he was also her husband of five centuries, so therefore he was her fool, and therefore her problem to deal with. The only saving grace was that he had been touched by Amalek - one of the Immortal Firsts - that had to be worth something.

Jacob's rise to the highest Cytheran office a mere fifty years ago had come as a shock to many - but not to her. He'd always been ruthless in his pursuit of power, but never obvious. Others didn't see the darkness lurking behind his former blue eyes, a darkness he never let show in the Cytheran and Tunaki realms, but always managed to surface when he stayed too long among the Toppers; rising like hunger pangs ignored too long. She'd known of his dark streak long before they were wed - but like her human female counterparts, she was convinced in time she could reform him, that the good she knew buried deep within him would eventually overshadow his taste for... other things.

That conviction in her ability to illicit change wasn't as solid as it used to be.

Jacob seemed to possess an unquenchable thirst for inducing pain and suffering in others, and his willingness to compromise so much in achieving the means to do that at will - no, not necessarily the quest for power of freedom or power itself - it was his quest for pleasure that seemed to fuel him, and not the simple gratifications of wine, women and toys. Jacob hurt things, like a child tormenting a captured insect - but he'd never hurt her - much- and he'd never asked her to participate in his "hunts" over the centuries among the Toppers - not since their time in England over a century ago when his bloodlust had earned him the moniker of 'Jack the Ripper' in the local press. She shuddered at the memory of all those poor prostitutes - they'd never done anything to deserve his flippant cruelty, and his carelessness had caused them to flee the Topper lands once more for the safety of Redstone.

Her slippered feet moved silently along the polished red rock at the base of the spiral staircase, but not quiet enough to avoid the scrutiny of Joshallon, head of the Cytheran Guard who stood vigil at the caverns entrance. He was regaled in full battle armor: gold-plated, Tunaki-forged stone polished to a mirror finish that gleamed in the subdued light of the turquoise wall sconces.

Hair-thin bits of shadow danced between the reticulated seams of lustrous plate, and his gauntleted hands rested deceptively on the twin swords belted at his waist, a pair of sleeping vipers that had shed the blood of thousands. Joshallon was among the eldest of the Cytherans, had led the Cytheran Guard for centuries even before Elaina was born, and she still marveled at how Jacob had managed to sway the stolid warrior over to his radical path.

His deep hazel eyes gave no hint of emotion, staring at her indifferently from beneath a gilded helm festooned with a blood-red plume of Kenawak hair trailing down his back. The same helm he'd donned when training Spartan warriors eons ago, although the snow white beard that framed his massive chin had no doubt been a much darker shade then. He may have been ancient - even by Cytheran standards - but Elaina knew there were none living or dead who could best him with a blade, amongst any species.

She stifled a shudder and tried to put on her most imperious air. He may be an elder - but she was the wife of their Clan Chieftain, and therefore above his scrutiny - she hoped. He would have to be watched very carefully.

"He awaits you in the alcove, M'Lady," rumbled the aged warrior in a tone just loud enough to be heard without echoing through the vast passage. She flinched slightly, nodded curtly, never eyeing him directly and whisked by in a flutter of ruffling thistle-silk and vain indifference.

Why did Jacob insist that I come down to this vile killing ground, anyway? He knows I have no taste for blood, nor do I wish to be a part of any of his political schemings. We've discussed this at length - my role is best as the social face...

Her mental griping was cut off as she rounded the corridor and entered the vast cavern - unprepared for the immense horrors splayed out before her. Thousands of crosses holding the limp and bloody carcasses of Topper women covered the horizon, the coppery stench of blood and pungent tang of excrement and death wafting over her in vile waves. She gagged involuntarily, mistakenly took a deep breath through her nose to stifle the nausea, then vomited heavily as the rank stench overwhelmed her sensitive stomach. Hundreds of the Topper/Drakos hybrids scurried about beneath the dead, poking gory, elongated snouts riddled with teeth into open stomachs and putrefying remains, thousands of the infant brood chittering like a plague of human-skinned locusts at the clawed, reptilian feet of their Drakos parents.

She squinted through tears, leaning against the cool cavern wall for support and saw the closest of the ungodly beasts eyeing her hungrily as she heaved again and again. The creatures' skin was the ebony black of the native denizens of Sudan, and a pointed widow's peak of tight, coarse hair ascended between eerily intelligent eyes that eyed her like a wounded antelope stumbling into a pride of blood-hungry lions.